CAFFEINE NIG

CW00971504

FUNERAL
RITES

ALFIE ROBINS

Fiction aimed at the heart
and the head...

Published by Caffeine Nights Publishing 2015

Published in Great Britain by Caffeine Nights Publishing

www.caffeine-nights.com

British Library Cataloguing in Publication Data.

A CIP catalogue record for this book is available from the British Library

ISBN: 978-1-907565-86-1

Cover design by

Mark (Wills) Williams

Everything else by
Default, Luck and Accident

Also by Alfie Robins

Just Whistle
Reprisal
Snakes & Losers

For
Karina, Lee and Tanya.

Acknowledgments

One again I would like to thank my family for their support whilst writing this book. Also a big thank you to Darren E Laws, CEO of Caffeine Nights Publishing for putting his faith in the novel.

FUNERAL RITES

Chapter 1
The Day I Died

I've heard it said that when you die, you see your whole life passing in front of you. You are born and then you die, and you see all the relevant milestones that occurred between. A bright light at the end of a long tunnel beckons, and you are welcomed into the next world with open arms, but can anyone validate it? Certainly not me; I can only tell you the story of what happened when I died.

"Twinkle, twinkle, little star, how I wonder what you are..." The words to the children's nursery rhyme played over and over in my head as I lay collapsed in a heap on the warm cobbled road that runs beside the Hull marina. I—I remember lying there, staring up at the stars in the ebony night sky above me. I swear I was up there, swirling, dipping and diving like a shooting star in the velvet heaven above me. Then my eyes closed. I was sweating like never before, a cold sweat that chilled me through; my chest felt as if someone was squeezing the life out of me.

I could sense someone was there, I forced my eyes to open, and saw a woman, kneeling down on the cobbles next to me, her breath warm against my skin as she kissed me. I couldn't breathe and she kissed me again, there on the cobbles. I couldn't see her face, her long hair hung down, soft over my own, obstructing my vision, I could smell her perfume and I could feel her hands pushing down on my body. I tried to speak but my mouth wouldn't work, then she kissed me again. Who was she?

Again, my eyes closed.

***

I didn't know what was happening or where I was going. All I knew was that I was going somewhere. Then I arrived at my final destination.

'Hello, Son, it's good to see you. I wasn't expecting you quite so soon.' White, bright, white and bright everywhere, almost dazzling.

'Hello, Mam, I didn't know I was coming myself until I got here. You're looking well, all things considered.' I smiled; it had been a long time, almost fifteen years. I was just pleased to be somewhere.

'You've not changed a bit, Son, just older.'

'Happens to us all.'

'What do you think of the place?

'Not quite sure yet, I thought it would be a while yet before I saw you again.'

'It's always like this: quiet. They look busy down there, you planning on stopping?'

'I might just do that.' I looked down at was happening below, a nurse was leaning over the body, she had a nice arse. 'Is Dad here?'

'He's about somewhere.'

We both watched what was happening below. 'They're working hard down there.'

'Mam, where are you going?' She was fading in and out like the picture on an old television set. 'Don't go yet, I've only just found you again.'

'I'll hang on a minute or two; do you know what brought you here?'

'Not really, I'd been out for the evening with friends; next thing I saw was you.' All the time we were speaking I was aware of the voices below us, so I looked down again.

'No output!' Someone in green surgical scrubs shouted, he looked like a doctor. I watched as he took two pink-coloured pads and stuck them on the chest of the man who looked a bit like me. 'Charging to two-fifty. Clear.' The defibrillator whirled to life. 'Shocking!' The insulated paddles struck the chest.

Thud, the body jerked, arched and fell back to the bed.

I jumped myself; it was as if I'd put my finger into an electric socket.

'Still no output, shocking again, charging to three hundred. Clear!'

Thud. The body rose and fell once more at the touch of the paddles.

I grabbed my chest, it hurt so bad.

'Are you ok, Son?'

'I've felt better, Mam.'

'I'm really not sure you should be here.'

'Pupils fixed and dilated, we're losing him,' I heard the nurse with the nice arse say.

'Three mls of adrenaline.' The doctor grabbed the syringe from the nurse and plunged the needle deep into the chest. 'Prepare to shock again at three-fifty.' He withdrew the needle and dropped it into a tray, picked up the paddles once again and applied them to the chest.

Thud.

The pain was even worse this time, like someone hitting my chest with a sack full of bricks.

'Looks like you're going back, Son. Not your time.' She was fading.

'Mam—no—Mam it hurts, stay with me, Mam.'

The picture faded then went completely, she was gone.

Back in my body, I gasped for breath.

'He's back ... at least for now.'

***

My name is Harry Blackburn, most people just call me "H" and I'm a copper. I can remember it all now, well most of it. I'd just been out to dinner with an old friend and colleague, and his partner, good company, good food and even better wine; all in all we'd had an excellent time, we said our goodbyes and headed off home. I grabbed a taxi back to my apartment on the Hull marina.

It was such a nice evening I had the driver drop me off at the city centre end of the marina near the Monument Bridge, I fancied some evening air and a stroll to walk off the food. It was a warm evening with a mist starting to rise off the town centre dock, I remember walking along the quayside listening to the water slapping against the boats, and watching the navigation lights twinkling in the night. I was content. Without a care in the world, I ambled along, whistling to myself, thinking how good life was. Strange, I don't ever remember knowing how to whistle.

All change. Shit. Whamo! Pain in the centre of my chest, it was like I'd been hit by someone swinging a sack full of bricks into me. The pain didn't go away, my knees wobbled making my legs give way and I keeled over. I was gone, just a wrecked, panting heap on the cobbled road. I sensed someone else was near but I didn't know who, then the sounds of sirens filled the air, getting closer. The next thing I knew, I was laid out on a hospital trolley with lights speeding past above my head. Everything that happened after that is a virtual blank.

Four hours later, I woke up in the Critical Care Unit of Hull's Castle Hill Hospital wondering what the hell had happened. The nurse assigned to me told me that once they got me stabilised, they'd had to fit a stent in one of my clogged-up arteries. Apparently I was still only firing on two cylinders and needed a by-pass operation in the next few weeks once I'd recovered enough. One thing she did tell me surprised me: if the young woman hadn't found me when she did, I'd have been a goner for certain. I couldn't remember any young woman, only a nice perfumed smell. Strange, I do have a vague recollection of a figure walking towards me out of the shadows, a man I think, but that's it.

Now here's the thing: when I came round I do remember asking for a brew. Also I remember the first time I looked in the mirror and wished I hadn't, I was a bloody mess. I know I'm not the best looking bloke in the world, but even so I was shocked. My face looked even more haggard than usual and grey with it, even my eyes looked like piss holes in the snow; overall, it's fair to say I looked as crap as I felt.

As far as hospitals go, the Castle Hill Cardiac Unit isn't so bad, but me, I hate hospitals, always have done, I guess it's almost a phobia. I think it's got something to do with the antiseptic smell, white sheets and all those ill people. I've always considered myself one of the lucky ones, that was until my attack. I'd been fortunate enough never to have had anything more serious than a dislocated collar bone, and that was due to some useless twat of a postie on a bicycle not looking where he was going, he knocked me arse over tit.

I was lucky in some respects: due to my works medical scheme, I was fortunate enough to have a private room. I didn't have to share my space with any coughing, farting geriatrics. While I was incarcerated my visitors were few and far between, but then again I'm an unsociable bugger at the best of times and don't need much company. I don't have any living family as such—saying that, I do have a brother, but we don't keep in touch on account of me being the black sheep of the family—but that's a story that will save for another day.

On the plus side of things, I did have visits from work colleagues, Detective Sergeants Ria Middleton and Mike Quest. DS Quest is one of my oldest friends. Mike, or Questy as we call him, became a regular visitor during my confinement. He and his partner William are the blokes I'd been out with the night of my attack. In between visits, there was bugger all to do except watch television. Oh yes, I caught up on my reading—you know, all those books you promised yourself you'd read when you had a chance? Questy brought me in *The Crooked Beat,* a private eye yarn by Nick Quantrill, a Hull author. Good book, I'd recommend it. I believe he's got another one out soon; I'll have to keep an eye out for it.

I couldn't really explain how I'd been feeling since I opened my eyes in the recovery room. It was surreal: as if I was there and I wasn't. I couldn't quite put my finger on it.

***

They kept me hospitalised for what seemed like weeks when it was only just over seven days until the discharge papers were signed. When they did let me leave, they gave me a list of do's and don'ts an arm long and enough medication to start my own pharmacy. When I told them I lived on my own, the cheeky buggers wanted to refer me to social services! I ask you, meals on wheels and all that? I told them very politely to piss off.

Take it easy, the doctor told me, and avoid stressful situations.

'Doc,' I said, 'you do realise that I'm a policeman? Ninety percent of my life is based on stress.'

He shrugged his shoulders as if to say, "well that's up to you" and the lists went on, stop smoking, cut down on the booze, and get plenty of exercise. That didn't stop me going and buying twenty Embassy King Size as soon as I left the hospital.

Anyway, I got a taxi back to the apartment. I could hardly push the door open for the brown envelopes and junk mail that had mounted up on the doormat. There was a nice postcard from some Greek island among the debris on the mat.

"Hope you're soon feeling better" was written on the back. It wasn't signed, but all the same I stuck it to the fridge door with a magnet. There it came again, that feeling, I went through to the bathroom to freshen up a bit, I ran the tap and splashed some water on my face and looked in the mirror.

'You look like shit', I said to the mirror.

'There's no need to remind me,' I replied.

'If I was you, I would just follow the doctor's orders.' For Christ's sake, I was talking to myself now.

***

Over the next week or so, I started to get myself together. When I felt strong enough, I decided that maybe I should make the effort and start my new healthy living regime. Every morning after a mug of builder's and a breakfast of "delicious" muesli, I began walking round the marina. It's a fair distance if you go all the way around. I took things easy, an easy stroll at first and built up to a bit of power walking—well, power walking by my standards.

You know it was strange, I'd lived in the apartment for around three years now and I hardly knew my neighbours, yet after a few days I was having conversations with neighbours and boat owners alike. I was even invited for coffee aboard the *Dancing Lady,* a restored 1930s fancy sea-going launch. I was on tenterhooks all the time I was on board: it was like a museum piece, nice people but Captain Derek and his wife Barbara were a bit on the posh side for a common copper like me.

With a plastic phallic symbol stuck between my lips to suck on, and with extra aid of three thousand or so nicotine patches to ease the cravings, I'd ditched the fags, almost. I still had a crafty one out on the balcony, that was when I could evade that voice telling me not to, but let's be honest, it wasn't going to do me much harm anyway. The booze, I thought I'd save that for another day: can't deprive my body of too many toxins, not that it matters.

It was August when I'd started my morning constitutionals around the marina, fine summer mornings with blue skies and sunshine. Wearing a very unfashionable track suit that I'd found at the back of the wardrobe, I started to pound the cobbles. Summer didn't last long and soon gave way to autumn, with cool breezes and falling leaves. As my fitness levels began to rise, so the sky started to lose its brightness; grey clouds, winds and showers soon followed. November was particularly bad, with exceptionally early morning frosts and biting winds. The deterioration in the weather continued and December was atrocious, the wind had done a turnabout to blow from the East, howling down the Humber estuary, bringing snow from Russia. I'm ashamed to say, on the bad days my trainers stayed by the door.

The one good thing to come from my absence from the office was that my immediate boss, DI Prosser, had decided to call it a day and agreed to take early retirement: the lazy sod is only 48 years old.

No love lost there.

Before my illness I was a Detective Sergeant, then DI Prosser—or the Tosser as we called him behind his back—went on sick with a bad case of haemorrhoids. The result being I was made up to Acting Detective Inspector. My big boss, Detective Chief Inspector Stan Fellows, told me the Tosser's retirement was due to personal and health reasons. As far as I knew, the lazy bugger only had something wrong with his arse; still I was glad to see the back of him. So was the rest of my team.

That's when I got the confirmation of being promoted to the full rank of Detective Inspector.

Chapter 2
The Policeman Goes Back To Work

Once I was feeling up to it, I made a point of becoming a regular visitor to the nick, to keep my face in the frame so to speak. My nick, Braemar Street, is along Hessle Road, not far away from the old St. Andrew's Dock. When I was a lad, Hessle Road was row upon row of back-to-back terraced houses, streets with names such as Constable, Eton and Harrow. This area of the city had been home to the country's largest fishing fleet. Most of the streets had gone now or been renamed, and St Andrew's Dock, the old fish dock, had been filled in and re-developed with large retail units, furniture stores and the like. A few of the old buildings were still standing—not as a tribute to the past, just that they hadn't been demolished yet. At one time, there was talk of converting the old Lord Line building into a heritage centre. You never know, it may happen, the day when the pigs fly overhead.

My visits to the station gave me a good chance to have a bit of a catch-up with the lads and to keep updated from the boss. Anyway with the doctor's agreement, and Stan's of course, it was decided I'd work myself back in gradually, you know, just do a couple of hours in the afternoon to get myself in the swing of things, and build it up from there.

So there I was, one stent and a double heart by-pass operation, and four months later I was back on the job full time. The first week after Christmas was my first full week back in the driving seat, literally, as well as at the station. What a day to pick to go back to work! It snowed, and did it snow! The city almost ground to a standstill as everyone left their cars at home and took to the few buses that were running, but not this silly bugger, I took the car.

At the nick, I shared a small office not much bigger than a broom cupboard with DS Ria Middleton, I've already mentioned her. While the Tosser had been on his sick leave, I'd been offered the use of his much more spacious office, but I'd refused; my excuse was that I was only an Acting Inspector and besides, I was used to sharing. It's good to have someone to bounce ideas off and the like, but now I'd had a chance to think it over I'd changed my mind about the office; a bit of privacy might be welcome.

I opened the door and burst into the broom cupboard. 'Morning, Sergeant. Not making a brew, are you?' The office was just as it had been before my sick leave, only a damn sight tidier.

'Harry, you're back then?' Ria said as she spun around on her chair and gave me a welcoming smile. Nice.

'Fully fledged Detective Inspector Harry, if you don't mind.'

'Straight up? All official?'

'Want to see my warrant card?' I made a big show of fishing about in my jacket pocket.

'No need, *sir*, I believe you.' Big emphasis on the "sir"

'Now look here, Sergeant, if you go and make me a mug of tea, I'll give you special permission to keep calling me Harry.' Ria knows I how like my tea, nice and strong so that you can almost stand a spoon up in it.

'If that's all it takes, I'm on my way.' She headed out of the office shaking her head, she always does that. 'Good to have you back, by the way,' she called from the corridor with her back to me.

I sat down in my leather chair, which was wedged between the wall and my desk. I looked around at the cramped space. It would be a shame to leave the sanctuary of the cupboard. It was all so familiar with its two desks crammed into a space hardly big enough for one. I felt light in the chair as if I was sat on air; it was far more comfortable than I remembered.

Ria and I had shared this *room* for a long time. I made a decision. Yes, I'll move into the Tosser's old office, but I was buggered if I was going to leave my chair: it had taken me years to get it this comfortable. I'd had some memorable times in this office, they'd usually been jokes at someone else's expense and occasionally mine.

'Thanks for that,' I said as Ria put the mug down on the desk. I shifted uneasily in my seat and broke the news. 'I'm off.'

'What? You've only just come back, are you not feeling too good?' She looked genuinely concerned.

'No you silly bugger, I'm moving into the DI's office, all proper.'

'Does that mean I get to inherit *all* this space to myself?' She looked quite pleased as she waved her arms around her.

'At least you could try to look a bit disappointed at me going,' I joked.

'Yes, well, I am, but—' she stammered.

'Quit while you're ahead, and bring me up to date.'

Before the conversation had much chance to go any further, my desk phone rang. During my sick leave Ria had become used to answering the phone, so the race was on to pick up the handset. She beat me, then gave me one of those looks and passed the receiver across. 'Blackburn.' It was DCI Stan. 'What can I do for you, sir?' I looked across to Ria and raised my eyebrows. 'Right, ok, give me five minutes and I'll come through.' I'd been summoned, I don't know what he wanted but I wasn't going to waste a good mug of tea, so I finished off the brew. 'Hold the fort. Stan wants a word, back in a bit.' Ria had her back to me and waved her hand in acknowledgement as I squeezed past her chair.

DCI Fellows is by and large a good bloke, he's a bit strict on rules and regulations, but then all senior management are, aren't they? I knocked on the door and walked in. He was sat behind his antique polished mahogany desk and the room smelled of beeswax and quality furniture. I won't say he's a vain bloke but he does have more than a couple of photographs of himself fixed on the wall. Even though he's a big man, Stan is one of those types you could dress in charity shop and he'd still look like an advertisement for

Armani. It's a shame about the shiny bullet head and the big lump of fat on the back of his neck that disappears into his shirt collar. Me, I'm the opposite; no matter what I wear, I always look like a sack of spuds.

'Harry, take a seat.' I already had done. 'Never change, do you Harry? Anyway, it's good to have you back holding the reins.'

'Thanks.'

He seemed genuine, Stan's not usually one for compliments. 'It's really good to be back.' We go back a long way Stan and me; at this point I usually start taking the piss, but not today. 'What can I do for you?'

'It's more what I can do for you.' Here it comes. He's making pyramids with his fingers, now he's picked up a pile of already tidy papers and re-tidied them again into tidy piles. I was worried. Then his face broke into a broad fat smile and he spoke.

'We have had a directive from Headquarters, which has been passed on to me to initiate.'

He looked like the cat that'd got the cream. Beaming from ear to ear, with the wrinkles running up his forehead, and regrouping on the top of his bald head, he looked a bit like one of those bald wrinkly designer cats, only smiling.

'Go on, I'm listening.' I stretched out my legs, trying to be casual, while all the time I was really on a knife-edge.

'As you are aware, your last investigation involved some assistance from Her Majesty's Customs and Excise, and it wasn't what could be called a resounding success.'

Very formal; it sounded as if he'd been rehearsing this speech for some time. As if I needed reminding about the case—it had been a fiasco. The result had been the death of two young women, one with a broken neck, the other overdosed with a stomach full of heroin-filled condoms. Oh yes, she was subsequently butchered and gutted like a fish to retrieve the haul. If that wasn't enough, her boyfriend was the victim of a hit, and was then murdered in his hospital bed. It didn't bloody end there either, the best witness we had was murdered while on remand in HMP Hull. No, I'm not finished yet, to add the icing on the cake, the man we thought responsible for all the mayhem headed off to the sun, before we, the team, had chance to arrest him. '*Here we, go,*' I thought, '*they're shipping me out, nobody to blame but myself for being an incompetent twat.*' I sat back in my chair and let him carry on, waiting for the axe to fall.

'But,—' he was enjoying it, 'saying that, the powers that be are, overall, duly impressed with your general clear-up rate.' Bloody hell, if a debacle like that could impress them, there was hope for me yet. 'We've been selected to spearhead a new initiative.'

'Bloody hell, there's a lot of big words there Stan. What's this new initiative?' Now I knew I wasn't to be booted out, put out to pasture, or, even worse, tied to a desk, I tried to show some enthusiasm. I was getting cramp in my arse and started shifting in my seat as he carried on.

'In certain circles, the Braemar Street Police Station is thought of as a backwater.'

'Can't argue with that,' I said. He obviously didn't like the comment, I could tell by the way he frowned and raised his eyebrows, making his wrinkly skin go all the way up his bald head. I kept watching, expecting the ripples to go right over the top.

'That's as maybe, Harry, but Braemar Street is now well and truly on the map, we've been selected to house the YPSIU.'

'That's a new one on me, Stan. What is this YPS— when it's at home?

'Yorkshire Ports Serious Incident Unit.' He was beaming again.

'Where do I come into the scheme of things?'

'Following a meeting between the Assistant Chief Constable, the Detective Superintendent and myself, it was decided you are the most suitable candidate.'

'Candidate for what?'

'To head up the new department. What do you think? Coffee?' He picked up the phone and had a word with his secretary Miss Prim and Proper.

'Bloody hell,' was all I said. Things like this didn't happen to a copper like me, especially at my time of life. Stan carried on, he sounded as if he was reading from an autocue as he gave me a rundown on things. I kept my gob shut and let him carry on. Once he'd finished his spiel he sighed, visibly relaxing and letting the wrinkles drop back down his face. Miss Prim and Proper brought in the coffee seconds after he finished speaking; she must have been stood outside the door with a tray ready and waiting. She put the tray down on Stan's desk, smiled at him and ignored me.

'Shall I pour? Any biscuits?' She gave me a disgusted look.

Apparently, if the initiative was successful, it was to be rolled out to other major ports and airport towns and cities around the country. No pressure then. Why the bloody hell had they picked me, I asked myself? I reckoned it must be because I was one of the expendables: if it all went tits up, I'd be on my bike.

'Nice coffee this, Stan,' I said as I sipped. For the next half an hour we talked through the strategies and logistics of the proposal. I was warming to the idea... slightly.

'Decision time, Harry. What do you think, are you ready for a new challenge?'

'I've got a couple of questions before I commit myself.' Commit myself! I reckoned I should be committed for taking it on.

'Go ahead; I'll answer what I can.' He looked pensive, he knew me well.

'Where's the team to be based?'

'I've already said, here at Braemar Street.'

'Not much space; whenever we have a major operation we're knackered, it happens every time.' The last major incident, we had to take over the conference room.

'No problem, I take it you *are* aware of the building work that's been carried out during your absence?' I don't know if he was being sarcastic, it wasn't as if anyone could miss it. I just nodded in response. 'It's the new YPSIU suite.'

YPSIU! What a bloody mouthful, it didn't look like I would be moving into the Tosser's office after all.

'The team, how many bodies?' I asked.

'Obviously you will be SIO, the team will comprise one Detective Inspector, two Detective Sergeants, four Detective Constables, with uniform as and when required.'

No change there then, just the same manpower.

'The team, my choice?'

I thought I'd be pushing my luck with this one.

'Entirely your choice...within reason.'

'DS Mike Quest, I'd like him assigned.' Questy had been temporarily seconded to my team for our last major cock-up. When the case was suddenly drawn to an unsatisfactory conclusion, he'd been returned to Regional Headquarters down Clough Road.

'Consider it sorted. I suggest you go away and have a think about who you want and the extra resources you think you may need.' Bloody hell, it was like giving me an open chequebook. Then he hit me with the bombshell.

'One more thing before we finish, we're also integrating a Customs and Excise Officer into the team, who will be your liaison contact with the Customs and Border Control people.'

This was a bolt from the blue and needed some serious thinking about: was I up to it in my current state of health? We were to take on the extra responsibility, and still be lumbered with the regular bread and butter work of a busy CID office. No matter how it was dressed up, it was just a way of using minimum input to achieve maximum output. Nevertheless, it called for another brew, so I headed to the canteen for a mug of builder's and one of those skinny latte things for Ria.

I don't know why, but every time I walked into the bloody canteen my shoes began to squeak, it was so annoying, never anyone else's, just mine. I'd got the squeak sussed by now though, I just walked with a purpose straight to the counter and avoided any eye contact with the buggers so they didn't take the piss. I was a bit disappointed when I got there, Bren the canteen manager who, I must admit I did fancy a bit, must have been having a day off. According to her name badge, the young lass behind the counter was called Jenna. She was a skinny little thing, a cross between a Goth and a punk, really weird looking, almost ghoulish with her white make-up. Nevertheless, after a quick chat she proved to be pleasant enough, even if she wasn't very health and safety conscious with all her piercings. Armed with our brews, I headed for the broom cupboard, squeaky shoes and all.

***

'Cheers, Harry,' I passed across Ria's mug. 'I thought maybe you'd got lost. Been with the DCI all this time?'

'Yeah, well, here's a story—and I've got a proposition I'd like to run by you,' I said as I plonked down in my seat.

'I've told you before, "H", I'm not that sort of girl,' she said as she spun around on her chair. She's not very good with jokes, but I laughed anyway just to be polite.

'Ha, ha, very funny. Just listen to what I've got to tell you.'

***

There was no getting away from it, I had plenty to mull over, and on top of that I was starving, so I decided to call it a day and head off home. The weather was still crap, it was sleeting like a bastard, but I managed to park right outside of the apartments and made a run for it and reached the door without slipping into the marina. In line with my fitness regime, I took the stairs rather than the lift. After all, I was only going to the first floor.

Silence as I opened the door, just as I like it. It was time to raid the ever-depleting stock of the freezer and liberate a Mark and Sparks microwave prawn curry. I admit for a convenience meal it hit the spot. No beer, mind, just a couple of mugs of tea. Promises, promises, they never last do they? Just the one won't hurt I told myself, and that's all I did have, a small tot of Jamaica's finest, Appleton's dark rum. Nursing my drink, I sat in my chair watching the micro world of the marina through the French doors and had one of those conversations with myself.

'YPISU, how do you feel about it?'

'Ok, I suppose, new challenges and all that.'

'You don't think you're taking too much on, all considered?'

'You mean at my age?'

25

'I was more thinking along the lines of your dodgy ticker.'

I let my eyes close and drifted into the surreal. The sky was exceptionally clear, the snow had stopped, there was a crescent moon and the stars were as clear as I'd ever seen them. I swam with the stars; once again I swam in the air, dived down to within inches of the water's surface and lay on my back with my arms stretched out, floating, looking up into the heavens. I didn't have any recollection of going to bed, obviously I must have because I was tucked under my duvet when the alarm sprung into action at 6.30 a.m. Must have been the Appleton's.

Chapter 3
Police Times They Are A Changin'

Over the next few days it was still business as usual while the move took place. For a change, crime was on the light side as far as CID were concerned. Apart from the usual domestic disputes, the villains by and large tended to stay indoors. It was always the same when we got a bit of snow, but it was a different kettle of fish during the warmer months, the booze had a lot to do with it.

By Thursday the move was almost complete. I was the first to say, taken as a whole, it had been a quite painless experience. There was very little we had to take from the main building, as the majority of the furniture and cabinets were new. Needless to say, I made sure my battered leather chair made the move without any extra damage. DS Mike Quest—Questy—as usual timed it right: he turned up on Friday morning just as the move was almost complete. In all fairness, he did carry my chair across to the new building.

"Harry, no, remember your condition, remember what the doctor said—no heavy lifting."

The cheeky bugger, the bloody thing was on wheels, I only had to push it across the car park to my new office, and I stress, *my* office. Ria and Mike were to share a partitioned-off area at the far end of the new squad room.

***

I was trying to get things sorted when there was a knock on the office door, and I could see the silhouette of a young woman through the frosted glass door panel. She obviously wasn't one of ours or she'd have just barged in. This one stood and waited. I like good manners.

'Come in!' I must have sounded more like a ventriloquist's dummy as I was holding a nail between my clenched teeth and could only mumble. I was balancing precariously on the edge of the desk with a hammer in one hand and a framed picture of the Humber Bridge in the other, trying my best to hold the picture while deciding where best to hang it.

'Detective Inspector Blackburn?'

I glanced across and nodded. I couldn't help but notice she had shiny dark brown shoulder length hair, perfectly styled in a way that enhanced her oval face and structured cheek bones.

'Need some help?'

Good lass. I'd hoped she'd say that, I like teamwork.

'Grab a hold of this, will you?' I once again mumbled through my teeth. She put her briefcase on the floor and I passed her the picture, took the nail from between my teeth and wiped it on my trousers. 'Thanks, won't be a sec.' Tap, tap, the nail was in and she passed back the picture which I duly hung and climbed down from the desk, I might add without falling arse over tit.

'What do you think?' I asked as I stood back to admire my handiwork, but she smiled one of those patronising smiles. 'Well, now you know who I am, who are you?'

'Senior Customs and Excise Officer Ford.'

'First name?' I asked the slim brunette in front of me.

'Samantha.' She brushed away a stray hair from her face; I noticed she had piercing eyes, and nice legs.

She held out her hand. For a woman she had a bloody good grip, not one of those limp wrist jobs.

'Harry,' I said. 'Welcome to the team, fancy a brew, Sam?'

'I prefer Samantha, and coffee please, black.' That told me. I gave her a sideways look.

Then I stuck my head around the office door and shouted, 'Steevo, bring us a mug of tea and a black coffee, please.' I could see Sam-who-liked-to-be-called-Samantha, cringe as I shouted to DC Steve Wales.

We talked about what we were hoping to achieve with the new enterprise. Despite the hang up with her name, Sam-who-liked-to-be-called-Samantha seemed pleasant enough and appeared competent, I'd already checked her out.

According to her personnel file, by all accounts she was bright. It didn't mention how good looking she was.

When we'd finished our brew, I sent Steve Wales to find Ria and Mike. Mike had done a disappearing act but he tracked Ria down in the custody area and brought her back. I did the introduction thing and left them to it, so that Ria could give Samantha a quick tour of the main station building, toilets and that sort of thing, all girls together.

Twenty minutes later they duly arrived back, bearing a mug of builder's with my name on it.

'Right, Samantha,' I said, 'what I would do if I was you, is get into that squad room and find yourself a desk before the rest of the buggers get established.'

'Thanks, I'll do that.'

'They're a good bunch, you'll soon settle in.' She gave me that nice smile again.

***

I wouldn't admit it to anyone but after a full week back on the job I was knackered, the early mornings and regular hours had set me back a bit, so I knocked off early and headed home. Mind you, I suppose being back at work full time did have its good side, at least I was getting back into some sort of routine, or rut, depending on how you looked at it. An unmarried copper's diet is pretty much what you'd expect: even though I like to cook when I can, food is usually something from the freezer. Then I'd have my bath followed by a couple of cans of Boddingtons and nod off in front of the television or in my chair, facing out over the marina. Remember I said I'd leave the booze for another day? I'm still waiting for that day to arrive.

Anyway, I'd wake up bleary eyed around midnight razzing with myself for nodding off, again, and then head off to bed, very predictable for me. Well, bugger being predictable, I thought, I've worked my first full week for some months. The pub beckoned, it was, after all Friday night and I deserved a treat. On top of that, unusual for me, I was fed up with my own company, and sitting on my own in front of the television just didn't appeal. I reckoned I'd earned a couple or three pints.

I used to use *Ye Olde Black Boy* on the High Street in the old part of the town, but since I'd had my attack I'd been going to the nearer *Minerva*, by the former Victoria pier, right on the river front. Best of all, it was an easy stroll away down the quay and across the marina lock gates; it had become part of the route in my exercise regime, not visiting the pub but crossing the lock gates that is. I don't know why I hadn't made it my local sooner.

'Pint of my usual please, Jimmy,' I called out as I swung the pub door open.

'Since when did you have a usual?' Sarcastic bugger.

'Never mind the backchat, what's the weekend special?' The *Minerva* had revitalised itself by installing one of those micro-breweries, you know, one of those Real Ale pubs that brew their own beer on site and have their own weekly brewed specials. Jimmy was not only the landlord of the establishment, but also the brew master.

'Harry, it's all unique, made with these fair hands.' The clever dick waved his hands in the air; he was right of course, the beer was bloody good. I could never fault it.

'Just pull me a pint, something thick and dark.'

The good thing about the place was that it was out of the way: too far from the city centre for the young crowd and yobs to be bothered with. The main clientele of the *Minerva* were the lovers of Real Ale and it appeared to be somewhere a bloke could take his bit on the side away from prying eyes. There was always some couple sat in a corner holding hands.

With my pint in front of me, I perched on a high stool by the bar putting the world to rights with Jimmy, watched the rugby on the telly and nattered with the regulars. All in all, a pleasant evening was had.

About 11.30 p.m. and four pints of Special Chestnut Stout later, I decided to call it a night. As soon as I opened the pub door, the bar was engulfed in a stream of sleet, blowing straight off the River Humber.

'Shut that bloody door!' everyone yelled simultaneously, before I even had a chance to get outside, never mind shutting the bloody thing behind me.

Collar up, woolly hat and scarf on, I tucked my hands deep in my pockets and set off home. It was bloody cold, the freezing wind and sleet seemed to penetrate right through my coat and cut to the bone. I felt a little unsteady as the fresh air hit me, not pissed, just mellow.

The marina area where I lived used to be a hive of activity. Apart from being a busy commercial dock, the area had been the heart of the fruit and vegetable business. This part of the old town was undergoing massive regeneration, the new living alongside the old. On my way home from the pub, I passed by the streets that used to make up the old fruit market. It wasn't unusual to see the odd homeless person dossing down around here. Most times I tried to ignore them, if any of them did come on a bit aggressive I flashed my warrant card and that usually did the trick.

Tonight was different, I don't know why; perhaps it had something to do with the things that had happened to me lately. Instinct took over and made me look twice at the shadowy figure crouched in a dark door recess.

I went closer. I could see it was a young woman. She was huddled on the cold concrete floor in a dingy, stinking doorway. She didn't look like a happy bunny. I didn't go too close, you know what it's like with distressed young women, I didn't want her yelling rape or anything.

'What's happened, love? You ok?' I went forward cautiously and slowly kneeled down in front of her. I must have looked a bit like a dosser myself in my big coat and woolly hat. She was in a bit of a state. The clothes she was wearing—or not wearing—wouldn't have kept a coat hanger warm in the crap weather. Through the darkness I could see scrapes on her bare legs, and her face looked as if it had taken a punch or two. She had a bloody lip and her right eye was starting to close up nicely. Someone had given her a right seeing to. She cowered away from me as if she was trying to disappear into the wall, mumbling through her swollen lips. I couldn't make out what she was saying. I put an arm out and she flinched, so I backed off a little.

'I think you need a hospital, love. How about I call an ambulance?' I reached into my pocket for my mobile.

'No, no 'ospital, plis.' The accent was eastern European.

'Well you can't stay here all night, love. If you won't go to hospital, at least let me get you a taxi.'

'I ok. Please go, leave me alone.' With shaky legs she tried to stand but fell back against the wall.

'Look, I live just up there a bit.' I pointed across to my apartment block. 'Why don't you come with me and let's get you cleaned up.' I smiled, trying to give some reassurance. I couldn't just leave her there, could I? She seemed to weigh me up, and then she nodded.

I edged forward again and she let me help her to her feet. As she leaned in closer I could see the look in her eyes: she was frightened to death. I reckon she was thinking that maybe I was some punter going to give her another beating. She stiffened when I put my arm around her shoulders, then relaxed a little and leaned a bit further into me. The crap weather didn't help things as we tramped through the sleet and slid our way across the checker-plate decking of the lock gates. The cobbles were even worse, the same cobbled road I'd collapsed on. My apartment was in a converted nineteenth century warehouse complex, and as I opened the main door to the building I could tell she was unsure, I could feel her body stiffen again at my touch as I guided her into the residents' foyer and into the lift. The look on her face said it all. I could tell she was wondering what the hell she was doing there and I wondered the same myself.

Once we were in the apartment and the door closed behind us she stiffened, then when she realised I wasn't going to pounce on her she seemed to settle a little. My apartment was by no means a palace: two bedrooms, bathroom, a lounge diner and kitchen. It wasn't cold as the central heating was on but I switched on the gas fire anyway. I told the girl to make herself comfortable and went into the kitchen. I made myself a mug of tea and a coffee for her, automatically putting in milk and sugar. When I went back into the lounge she was sitting on the floor in front of the fire with her arms wrapped around herself. It was a real struggle trying to get her to talk, she was very reluctant to tell me anything about herself except her name was Kaja, Kaja Karubach and she was from Estonia. She was done in, so I decided not to push it.

'I ok now,' she said when she'd finished her coffee. 'I go now.' She stood and reached for her thin jacket.

'Home?' I asked.

'No home, go back work.' Could I let this girl go back into the night?

'Kaja,' I said. 'Look at you. You're not in any fit state to go anywhere, never mind going back on the streets.' Without putting my brain into gear I said, 'You can stay here tonight.' The fear in her eyes came back at the suggestion. 'Don't worry, you're safe. You can sleep in the spare room, ok?' I added quickly. The spare room consists of a bed settee, small wardrobe and computer desk, it doubles as my office. Thankfully she agreed, I gave her a towel and showed her to the bathroom, I heard the lock click into place.

'I hope you know what you're doing.' Jesus, I was talking to myself again.

'Of course I do, I think.'

'Trouble Harry, this looks like trouble to me. It can only end in tears.' I should really listen to myself, these things usually find a way of going arse over elbow.

What the bloody hell was I doing, bringing a working girl back to the apartment? And a very young one at that, she looked barely out of her teens. I poured myself a small tot of Jamaican rum and the taste of molasses burned its way down to my stomach. I drank it down, poured myself another and went and sat in my favourite chair, a big leather recliner facing through the balcony doors, watching the sleet as it turned to snow, creeping higher up the glass. No matter what the weather, I loved the view.

Twenty minutes later I heard the lock click on the bathroom door. I turned my head, the girl came out wearing my dressing gown. She looked even younger without the makeup, her blonde hair fastened high on top of her head wrapped in a towel, a purple bruise emerging around her right eye.

'You want Kaja?' she said as she opened the dressing gown wide. I could see fading bruising on her thighs and on her ribs below her right breast.

'Whoa!' I said. 'Fasten yourself up.' I was flustered and could feel myself colouring up.

'Then how else I pay you? I have no money.' She stepped closer.

'Kaja, there's no need, honest.' The heat around my neck subsided.

The girl wrapped the gown around her and sat on the floor in front of the fire again. I passed her a drink.

'No payment needed, ok? Understand?'

She nodded. 'What is your name?' She sipped her drink and grimaced as the rum went down.

'Harry. Harry Blackburn.'

'I like to stay please. You are a kind man, thank you, Harry.' She held the glass in both hands and sipped at her drink.

I went to the airing cupboard and brought out the spare quilt and a pillow. 'Anything else you need, help yourself.' I showed her to the spare room and put the bedding down on the sofa bed. 'I'm going to bed. You'll be alright?' She looked lost. I left her sitting on the floor in front of the gas fire.

I made sure my wallet and mobile phone came with me.

'She's trouble Harry. Trouble.' I told myself.

Chapter 4
The Gangster

John Shaw's the name, drugs is my game. Not funny? Ok, I'm a businessman and look after the business interests of a good friend of mine who now lives in a warmer climate. My main function in life is to oversee his UK interests, the general day-to-day running of his UK operation. I am one of those people who generally keep a low profile, delegation is my motto. What's the saying, "why have a dog and bark yourself?" Well that's what I tend to do. I show my face periodically as and when needed. This was one of those occasions.

I had to pay a visit to one of the business premises, a "house" down Coltman Street. We were moving some merchandise to help keep the cash flow ticking over and all that, you know how it is. Coltman Street, a side street off Hessle Road, used to be quite a posh area well before my time, with tall three storey houses owned by prominent locals in the fishing industry. But now? Well, it was mainly flats, some let out to nurses from the Hull Royal Infirmary, but also many being owned by slum landlords with DSS tenants. It would be fair to say the street had gone right down the Swannee.

The house I was visiting wasn't one of our best establishments, but it did have a good regular turnover that helped to keep the coffers full. There was plenty of parking space, so I was able to park the car out front of the mid-terraced house. The front door opened straight onto the street. Shit! I only had to walk three feet and I nearly went arse over tit on the ice. '*Stay cool,*' I said to myself, got myself together, knocked on the door and was let in by a colleague. The place fucking stank, it was rank, hey I'm a poet. Corny.

I'd told the bloke who looked after the premises, Alexei, to get the girls together and be in the downstairs living room for 7.30 p.m. Alexei was a Russian guy who acted as a minder-cum-nursemaid, to make sure things ran smoothly. He'd done as he was told, as the girls were all there waiting.

Now, I'm not a scary looking bloke, especially when suited and booted in my finest, quite presentable, but the girls always looked a bit apprehensive when they saw me. A few of the ladies in the house had been there a while and knew me —and those that did, knew I don't pay house calls without a good reason, I reckoned they thought one of them was going to get their arse kicked. I thought it best to put them at their ease, so I took some little plastic packets from my pocket and threw them among the empty mugs and beer bottles on the coffee table. Cocaine.

'Special treat for you, ladies.' A few of the sad cows started giggling as they reached for the packets. 'Enjoy,' I told them. 'You're all going to a party.'

'Where is party?'

There was always one gobby cow, wasn't there?

'None of your fucking business.'

'Then I not go to party.' The cheeky bitch picked up a packet of coke and tossed it back at me.

'Who the fuck do you think you are?' I looked towards Alexei for a name, I can't remember them all.

The girl was called Kaja.

'You will do as you're fucking told, whore.' Outwardly I tried to keep a calm front, but I was fuming. How dare she speak when not spoken to, let alone talk back at me.

I nodded to Alexei. He didn't need telling twice, he walked across the room, grabbed the whore by the hair and gave her a good, hard, back hander across the face. She was tough this one, no tears as she dropped to the floor with a trickle of blood coming from the corner of her mouth. Another girl, the one I was interested in, swiftly moved across to the whore and dropped to her knees. She knelt down and wiped the blood from Kaja's lip. They looked like sisters.

'Leave her,' I shouted at the girl and looked towards Alexei. Scared, she knew the score. He grabbed the jumped-up little scrubber by the hair again and gave her another slap. 'Enough, we don't want to put the punters off.' Scary? Well, he put the willies up me. I was still shaking inside with fury, clenching and un-clenching my fists.

Alexei could sense things. 'Come, have a drink, yes?' He reached for the vodka bottle on the table; he needed to calm himself down, never mind me.

I looked around at the other girls. There wouldn't be any more bother tonight.

'Not yet.' I was still looking at Kaja, the girl who had defied me. I walked across, she thought I was going to give her a slap, so cowered back and covered her face with her hands. She was surprised when I helped her to her feet. 'It's ok if you don't want to go to the party,' I told her, smiling, and she smiled back at me. I grabbed the top of her arm, squeezed until she winced with pain, then pulled her to the front door, opened it, and slung her onto the street. 'So, no party, no problem. You can get out there and earn your fucking keep.' I threw her bag out into the snow after her, it was like something out of *Oliver Twist*.

I went back into the room and gave them all the evil eye, although nobody dared make eye contact. Alexei passed me a glass of Polish vodka and I downed it in one, good stuff. The girls still looked frightened, and so they should. 'Time to go, ladies,' I said. 'Get a move on, shift your arses.' I stood and watched as they grabbed their bags and Alexei ushered them out of the house into the minibus. I could see the girl, Kaja, standing at the corner of Coltman Street and Hessle Road. I slammed the side door of the van shut and climbed into the front passenger side.

I turned to Alexei. 'You know where we're going?'

'Yes, no problem, my friend.' I was no-one's friend!

The only thing worse than a van full of giggling tarts, is a van full of giggling tarts high on cocaine.

'Right, quit the chatter you lot,' I shouted over my shoulder. No-one took a blind bit of notice; cocaine does that to you, so I'm told. Never touch the stuff myself.

Alexei took over. 'Reeta, get them to keep quiet, or you'll be out in the snow with your sister.'

Well, well, well. So, they were sisters!

Natter, natter, natter, all the way to the party. As I said, I would normally have left this to Alexei; getting roped in for one of these parties is *not* my ideal night out. Ok, the parties were a bit prestigious, especially this one, with more than a couple of influential people attending. The big thing about these get-togethers was that money never changed hands, they were by special invite only, a "you scratch my back and I'll scratch yours" sort of deal, no questions asked. A typical example of what I mean was, you never know when you might need help with planning permission, right? Or even need a question asked in the House of Lords, know what I mean?

If any of the guests wanted to express their gratitude to the girls by the way of a cash gift, all well and good, as long as me and the boss saw the lion's share, sort of like income tax.

Tonight was a bit special; we had a VIP visiting us from up North, we had to be on top form. Tonight was sale night.

The evening's little soirée was to be held in a substantial detached property in Kirkella, one of Hull's more expensive suburbs. You couldn't buy decent property here for less than 300k, not anything that was worth having. For these special nights we tried to keep the venues to ourselves until a couple of hours before, always on the move like, and we tried not use the same location too often.

Alexei pulled up at the electrically controlled gates and announced our arrival into the gate speaker phone. The girls were excited, bubbling, nice and high on the coke, and we pulled up right outside the front door.

I wished they'd keep quiet, but at least they all looked to be up for anything.

'Right girls, we here,' Alexei said. 'Put your knickers in your handbags.'

They all started to giggle again. Junkie whores.

I put a big smile on my face and turned in my seat. 'Right, laydeeze,' I said, looking from one girl to the other. 'Let's all forget the silly incident earlier in the evening and you all go and have a good time.' I put on a smile and followed the girls into the hallway. Reeta was the last girl, I grabbed her arm. 'Not so fast, you're coming with me.'

'Where are you taking me?'

I ignored her and led her down the hall. I could hear music coming from the main lounge as we passed.

'It's alright, Reeta, don't worry,' Alexei told her.

I wanted everything to run smoothly, there was a lot riding on this. If the buyer was satisfied, then we were in for making a lot of money from future deals.

***

The door to the games room was closed; I gave it a knock and waited, these people I was dealing with were not the sort of people who'd appreciate it if you barged in. A couple of seconds later it was opened by our host. He reeked of money, from his Armani aftershave to his Rolex watch. The buyer was already waiting. Reeta held back as I ushered her in.

Alexei put a hand on her shoulder. 'It's alright, Reeta, you'll be fine.' He pushed her forward. She definitely did look worried.

I knew the buyer from other transactions, one of the big players on the Tyne, he stood with the host for the evening next to the snooker table. To my right, five nervous girls stood in a line and I told our girl Reeta to join them. I shook hands with the buyer and had a quick word. He wasn't going to mess about; it was straight down to business.

Reeta stood at the end of the line of frightened looking girls. The buyer walked across to study the merchandise. 'Take off your clothes,' he told them. Reeta looked towards me, I nodded. As quickly as they could, they undressed, letting their clothes fall to the floor. Once they were naked, he walked across to inspect the merchandise. The poor buggers looked terrified to death, as he walked slowly and carefully along the front of the row and then around the back, not speaking. They looked like shy schoolgirls, as they stood there trying to cover their bits with their hands, you wouldn't have thought they were hardened whores.

When he'd finished examining the merchandise he came back. We stood talking with our host, the buyer was making the right sounds and things were looking good.

Yes! We had a deal! I was a happy man.

Our host turned to face the girls. 'You and you, get dressed,' he told Reeta and another girl. 'The rest of you, out, NOW.' My girl looked frightened, as the others picked up their belongings and ran from the room, arses wiggling as they went.

A quick shake of hands and the deal was sealed with a large single malt.

The deal may have been done, but the buyer added a condition, he wanted me to deliver the goods, all the way to Newcastle. Tonight. Bloody hell, Newcastle, I know it almost as well as I do Hull, I've been there more than a few times with my boss. I told the buyer there was no fucking way I was travelling halfway up the country at this time of night and I'd take the girls first thing in the morning. He insisted it had to be tonight. I wasn't going to protest too much, I didn't want to lose the deal. Fuck.

I gave Alexei a shout, he grabbed hold of the other girl. Who the fuck she was I didn't know or give a toss. I took hold of Reeta by the elbow and we led them through the back of the house and pushed them into the back seat of a BMW 3 Series. Nice car.

'Do you need me to come with you?' Alexei asked me.

'Na, I can handle a couple of tarts,' I told him. In retrospect, I wished I hadn't been such a clever sod.

'Where are we going?' Reeta asked me, I ignored her. I pulled the BMW out of the drive and headed for the M62, my intention was to join the M1 at Ferrybridge and then head north.

'Please, where we going?' She was persistent.

'Newcastle.'

'Where is Newcastle?'

'Never fucking mind, you'll see when we get there.'

'What about Kaja, is she coming?'

I glanced in the rear view mirror. 'Don't be fucking silly, I'm not taking you on a day trip to the seaside.'

'Stop car, I not want to go to Newcastle.'

'Never mind Newcastle, you'll end up on the fucking streets like your sister if you don't shut your fucking trap.'

I glanced in the rear view mirror again, they looked worried. So they should, there's some right rough fuckers up in Geordieland.

Chapter 5
The Policeman Makes A Discovery

One good thing that came out of my promotion was that I didn't work weekends. Ok, there was always the exception to the rule, like when there was a major incident, but this Saturday was all mine. I didn't set the alarm clock; I woke up at just gone 8 a.m.

Bloody Hell! There was a girl sleeping in my spare room!

I pulled on my jogging pants and a top and went through to the lounge. The door to the spare room was slightly open. I glanced in and to my surprise, she was still there, fast asleep. I had it in my mind she'd have done a runner with the family silver—that is, if I'd had any.

Of course I didn't know the girl from Adam, but all the same I reckoned she needed her sleep so I left her be. I tiptoed around as much as I could, shut myself in the kitchen and tried not to rattle too many pots as I made myself a brew. With my tea and my fags, I went out onto the balcony for a nicotine fix. Needless to say it was bloody freezing and I didn't stay very long. Shivering, I went back into the kitchen. I was stood leaning against the radiator warming my arse, mulling things over, when Kaja came in from the spare bedroom rubbing her sleepy eyes, wearing my dressing gown again. Despite the purple bruise around her eye, the girl looked a damn sight brighter, and somehow she looked familiar, as if I'd seen her before.

Kaja didn't say much over breakfast, she was still secretive. The only new thing I learned about her was that she was twenty-four years old, and came to England with her younger sister Reeta a year ago. Where they lived or how she came to be working the streets, she wouldn't say and I didn't push the subject. Breakfast consisted of tea, toast and small talk, and when it was over, she went back into the bedroom to dress and reappeared in her street clothes. She thanked me for letting her stay the night.

'Are you sure you'll be ok?' I asked. She said she would.

I telephoned a taxi for her and gave her ten quid for the fare, then I passed her one of my business cards. Until then she had no idea I was a copper, so she was well surprised. And I was well surprised when she gave me a nice kiss on the cheek as she left.

After the girl departed, I thought I'd better make the effort and get back to my exercise routine. Trainers on, so, wrapped up in my scarf, woolly hat and gloves I set off on a jog, slipping and sliding around the marina. When I reached the river front I could see the tide was in, the Humber looked seriously dangerous as the swell bashed against the timber legs of the pier. Despite the atrocious weather, there were still three dickheads wrapped up like they were ready to go on an Arctic expedition, fishing in the Humber. I can't understand it myself, dangling a worm on a hook into the murky water trying to catch an eel or some inedible fish. I like mine to come ready battered and fried with chips.

The rest of the weekend passed without any excitement, no calls from the nick, it was pretty boring really. I kept hoping there would be some crisis, but the call never came. Other than the jogging, I didn't venture any further than the *Minerva* for a pint or two, it was too bloody cold. On my travels I kept an eye open for Kaja, but I didn't see her, probably never would again.

Chapter 6
The Policeman Has A Visitor

'Morning, Harry. That was good timing, I've just put the kettle on. Have you seen our new kitchen?' This did surprise me, Ria is hardly what you would call the domesticated type, but she was well impressed with our new facilities, excited even. Sad. 'We've even got a microwave.'

I walked away shaking my head and went to *my* new office. 'Questy in yet?' I asked when she brought in my drink.

'He's introducing Samantha to uniform.' She sat down without being asked to, not that I was bothered, we went back too far for that.

'At least she's safe with him.'

'Harry!' She said and gave me a scolding look.

'Well she is, I'm only stating the obvious.' DS Quest had recently dropped the bombshell on me that he was gay. I'd been best man at his first wedding, for goodness sake. He'd had a further two wives since then and I didn't have a bloody inkling, and it seems, neither had any of his wives. 'What do you know about people trafficking?'

'In what context?'

'Girls brought over from Eastern Europe used in the prostitution racket.'

'Probably only know the same as you, that it's rife in Hull as much as in most cities, any special reason?'

'Not sure yet. Nice tea this, you haven't lost your touch.' I sipped at the brew. I didn't see any point in anyone knowing about my overnight guest.

'Mind you, since you've been on sick leave, Vice have been having a purge on unlicensed massage parlours, but as soon as they shut one down, another springs up.'

'Tell me about it; there's one not a bus ride away from my apartment, on the other side of the marina near Holy Trinity Church. Do me a favour and have a word with Customs Samantha about it, let me know what you come up with. And keep it discreet.'

She inclined her head to the side. 'What's it all about?'

'I'm not quite sure yet, but when I am you'll be the first to know, so keep it to yourself for now.'

'Will do.' She stood up to leave. 'By the way...' She left it hanging there.

'What?'

'It's good to have you back at the helm.'

I smiled and picked up my mug. Questy was passing my window and when I gave him a wave, he stuck his head around the door. I nodded towards the spare chair for him to sit down.

'What can I do for you, "H"?'

'Your new partner.'

'What new partner?' He gave me a funny look and did that thing where he touches the hair resting on his shirt collar. All these years and he still has a *Beatle* hair cut; mine went a long time ago.

'Sam-who-likes-to-be-called-Samantha, I'm going to pair you up.'

'I've no problems with that, she seems ok from what I've seen so far.'

'I haven't made my mind up about the situation yet and I've a few reservations. We don't know how this thing with Customs Samantha is going to work out, if at all. We hardly know how they operate from the far end of a fart, and that certainly doubles from Customs' point of view.' I hesitated slightly. 'So, you're ok with it?' He nodded. 'Right, we'll have a brew shall we?' He got the message and went to the kitchen. I'd have to cut down on all the tea: there was no wonder I was always wanting a piss.

Questy duly came back and I passed him a report I'd received from the Customs people. 'I reckon this should be right up Samantha's street.'

He took the folder from me and scanned through it.

45

'Petty smuggling and motor bike spares! Come on Harry, I'm a bit past something as piddling as this.'

'Now don't get stroppy, finish reading the report before you blow a gasket. Customs reckon this petty smuggling is worth over five million quid a year in lost revenue.' This seemed to satisfy him. 'Besides, it'll give you a chance to see how Samantha operates.'

The other reason for pairing the two up, which I didn't mention to Questy, was there was no doubt she was a good looking young woman, and I didn't want the likes of DC Steve Wales and his mates constantly sniffing around her. At least with Questy's newly found sexual preferences, he wouldn't get side-tracked and they'd get on with the job. Or was I thinking she might turn him? I smiled to myself at the thought.

***

Come Thursday evening, the drive home was horrendous, it was snowing like a bastard and the windscreen wipers struggled to keep the screen clear. As I drove up to the apartment block, I could see someone lingering in the lee of the building, trying unsuccessfully to keep out of the snow. It was Kaja.

'Trouble at mill,' I said out loud.

I parked the car on the quayside and walked across. At least she was more suitably dressed for the weather than last time I'd seen her, wearing jeans, high heeled leather boots and a short faux fur jacket.

'Kaja,' I said, 'I wasn't expecting to see you again this soon. You waiting for me?' Stupid question, who else would she be waiting for?

'Harry, my sister Reeta, she not come home.' Tears started flowing. This was all I needed, I'm not very good when it comes to that sort of thing.

'Come on, let's get inside, you look nithered.' She gave me a funny look: I don't think she'd heard the term before, 'it means freezing cold,' I told her. She was wet through, the sleet was running down her hair and face. It was warm inside, as the central heating had kicked in, so I gave her a

46

towel to dry herself off, while I hung her jacket over a radiator and then put the kettle on. Once the kettle was boiled and the tea made it was almost déjà vu as we sat at the kitchen table. I sat nursing my brew, I didn't say much, just sat quietly and gave her some time to pull herself together. When she was composed, I saw her body lift and drop as she took a deep breath and began.

'Harry, you are policeman, yes?' She was getting her composure back.

'For my sins.' The girl didn't have a clue what the expression meant. 'Never mind, start at the beginning and tell me what's happened.'

Kaja went on to give me the full story of how they arrived in the UK and how she and her sister ended up working the streets. The story was familiar and not a pretty one; anyway, to cut to the chase they shared a house on Coltman Street with four other girls. When Kaja arrived home on the Saturday morning after staying at my place, her sister hadn't come home from a party on the Friday night, nor had she turned up since.

'I take it you have checked with all of her friends?' I asked.

'We have no friends, just girls in house, we look after each other.' Sad.

'I have to ask you this. The girls in the house, you are talking about prostitution?' I could tell she was embarrassed by the way she cast her eyes down and nodded.

'Does anyone else live in the house with you and the girls?'

'Alexei, he lives in basement flat.'

'And what does he do?'

'Alexei, he look after girls who work in house. If girls have trouble, Alexei come.'

This was a bit odd: if the girls worked in a brothel, how come I'd found Kaja beaten up on the streets? I asked the question.

'How did you come to be working the streets Friday night?'

47

'All girls have to go to big shot's private party; I say no, not want to go.' She pointed to her black eye. 'He make me work on streets.'

'Who?'

'Boss man, he came around to take girls to party.'

'This boss man, does he have a name?'

'I only know him as Boss.'

'And your eye—was that Alexei?' I gestured to her purple bruise and she nodded. Bastard; he sounded a right twat. 'Reeta, she went to the party?'

'Yes, he said he beat me again, so she went with them.'

'You say no-one has seen her since?'

'No, girls say she went into different room, never saw her again.' She started to cry again, I passed her a box of tissues. 'Harry, you find her, yes?'

'Tomorrow morning, you come into the nick?' She looked a bit nonplussed. 'The police station, ok?'

'No police station! Just you help.' It was obvious she had a big distrust of the police.

'Look Kaja, this is something I can't do by myself. You have to come into the station.' The girl nodded. 'It's going to be ok. I'll do what I can.'

'Thank you, Harry, thank you.'

It was a right bloody kettle of fish but what else could I do? I couldn't let her down. Right?

'You hungry?' I asked. She was good at nodding. 'Right, you know where the kitchen is, you make us a hot drink and I'll go and get us a takeaway.'

When I got back from the takeaway Kaja had made herself at home; it made a change having company. Two glasses of wine later she'd mellowed a little and began to tell me how come she and her sister ended up in England. It was a familiar tale, they'd found jobs in the UK with an escort agency via the internet. These sites have a lot to answer for. They'd checked it out and had been told it was a legitimate licensed business and they would earn around £300 a week, leaving them enough to send a little back home. No money was wanted up front. This should have been a warning sign. The girls had been supplied with air tickets and student visas at a cost of £2,000 each, the repayment would be by a small amount deducted out of their wages each week, or so they thought.

They were greeted at Heathrow Airport by a happy, smiling young woman who told them of the wonderful life they were going to have in England. She led them out of the concourse to a waiting minibus full of other young women, all friends together. Once they were clear of Heathrow Airport it was a different matter though, their passports and money were taken from them. The name of the game soon became clear; they were to work in a massage parlour, a knocking shop by any other name. They'd been well and truly suckered in and trapped. Kept under lock and key as virtual prisoners, they were used and abused. Gradually, as they conformed, they were allowed a little freedom, but still very little money, no passports and nowhere else to go. They had no hope of liberty. "Ok," you're thinking. "Why didn't they just run away?" Simple, threats and promises of danger to their families in their own countries.

The wine continued to flow and I explained how I saw the situation. Now that the wheels were going to be set in motion to make it official, there was no going back. My first piece of advice was to not go back to the house as things would start to get messy. It was getting late, so I once again offered Kaja the use of the spare room, she declined the offer and against my advice insisted on returning to the house in case Reeta turned up.

I told her to try not to worry and we'd sort it in the morning. What a night, and what a can of worms had been opened.

'Trouble with a capital "T",' it looked like I could be right. But what was I supposed to do, say "sorry I can't help"? Ok, so I'm a soft touch, and a sucker for a pretty face.

***

My alarm clock woke me at 6.30 a.m., the heating hadn't come on for some reason and it seemed chilly even for me. I didn't bother with breakfast but thought I'd grab something when I got to the station. I made do with a coffee and a couple of fags on the balcony while looking out over the marina; it was still frozen in parts with just a dusting of overnight snow laying on the ice. The drive in to work was uneventful but I'd nearly gone arse over tit on the ice in the station car park. I punched the security code into the rear door of the main station building and went in. My stomach was starting to growl so I made a trip to the canteen my priority.

'Morning, Detective Inspector.' It was Bren, the manageress; I was half expecting the Goth girl.

'Good morning to you too, Brenda. You ok?'

'Brenda, very formal, Inspector.' She smiled. 'I'm fine, Harry. Never mind me, I'm not the one who's been in hospital, what can I get you?'

'Full English please and a mug of builder's.' She knows I like my tea so that you can stand a spoon up in it.

'You sure? All that fat, grease and who knows what's in the sausages, you should be thinking about your arteries. Wouldn't you rather have a nice bowl of healthy muesli?' I screwed up my face at the thought, but she did have a point. I compromised.

'Ok, scrambled eggs on toast…with a rasher or two.' I said, resting my elbows on the counter top.

'I know you've been ill, but what have I told you about leaning on my counter?' Bren scolded, I think she was smiling but couldn't tell because she'd turned her back on me.

'I'm still an ill man, surely you have some pity? You won't be smiling when I collapse of grease deprivation.'

'If you're that ill you'd better go sit down, I'll bring it over.' She passed me my tea.

I've known Bren for a long time now, we nearly went out on a date once, but as usual something came up and it never materialised. Who knows where it might have led to, all the free breakfasts a man could eat?

Still, I could always ask her again, maybe, when I've plucked up the courage. The eggs were a bit overdone but I wasn't going to say anything, tried that before.

'Good to see you've still got an appetite,' a voice said from behind me. It was Questy, with Sam-who-liked-to-be-called-Samantha tagging along. Things seemed to be working out between them. They'd been like Siamese twins since I'd paired them together. Samantha joined me at the table while Questy went for the coffees.

I picked up the bottle of brown sauce and applied a liberal dollop to try and rehydrate the scrambled eggs.

'Mike, Samantha, how's it going with the motorbike parts? Any joy?' I cut through the toast and speared a piece.

'According to the manifest, the parts were shipped from an address just outside Amsterdam. The Dutch police are checking it out,' Samantha told me. Questy reached across and pinched one of my rashers.

'You could lose a finger doing that,' I waved my knife at him. 'What about the delivery address?'

'A dubious-looking transport company in Selby. That's why we're here, to let you know we're going on a visit.'

'No problem. Just keep Ria briefed on your other cases before you go.' They finished their coffees and stood up to leave. 'And don't go mad with the expenses,' I shouted as they reached the door, to which I received the one finger salute from Mike. Then as an afterthought I shouted, 'How's William these days?'

'Fine, "H", he sends his regards.'

Ok, so Samantha hadn't turned him yet, early days. Mind you, he did that funny thing where he touched the nape of his neck were his hair meets the collar when he's on edge. Had he even told Samantha? If not, he'd have a bit of explaining to do if I'd put my foot in it with the William comment.

There was finally a bit of peace and quiet, as the last pair of uniforms left. I finished my breakfast and had a quick read of the *Daily Star*, not my choice of daily paper I might add, someone had left it on the table, honest. On my way out of the canteen I asked Bren for a skinny latte thingy for Ria.

These bloody squeaky shoes.

I made my way through the station and into the car park without being accosted by anybody and made the short walk across to the YPSIU building. What a bloody mouthful!

'Ria,' I said, holding up the drink as I went into the squad room. She gave me a nod and followed me into my office. Ria, being Ria, didn't wait to be asked to sit down, she did so anyway. At times I swear she thinks we are still sharing an office.

'Nice surprise, "H",' she said as she picked up the drink and held it between both hands. 'What do you want?' She knows me too well.

'Got a little story to tell you.' I sat back in my chair.

'I'm all ears.'

'I wouldn't say that.' She didn't laugh. 'Anyhow, listen to this.' I went on to describe the events which had started Friday evening. As usual, Ria made the right noises in the right places.

'This girl, Kaja, she stayed the night?' It wasn't really a question. Her voice seemed to go up an octave. 'It was a bit risky wasn't it?'

'Not really, I locked my bedroom door so she couldn't molest me.'

'I was more thinking of your wallet. How did you leave things?'

'She's coming in this morning,' I glanced at the wall clock, 'in about half an hour.'

'And don't you think Samantha should have been involved in this?'

'She will be, once we know a bit more. Let's just find out what we're about first.'

'So, the questions the other day about people-smuggling, this is what that was all about.' My turn to nod.

'Will you have a word with whoever is on the desk and tell them to bring the girl straight through when she gets here?'

'No probs, "H". Let's hope she doesn't get cold feet.' Ever the cynic.

Ria took the remainder of her skinny latte thingy with her when she left. I made a sneaky exit for a smoke in the car park, I always keep a packet of mints in my pocket these days to disguise the breath. I don't use the plastic smokers' shed out of principle; they might as well hang a sign on it,

"For the unclean only". Instead, I hide like a schoolboy. I went and sat in my car with the door open but didn't stay long, as it was bloody freezing. The sky had that heavy grey look to it, the snow didn't seem too far away. With my fag squashed out in the ice and mint in mouth, I returned to the office.

'Bloody cold out there,' I said as I walked in. Ria knew where I'd been and wrinkled her nose at the smell. Already sat by Ria's desk was Kaja, nursing a hot drink. She was well early.

'Good morning, Harry,' the girl said.

'And to you, Kaja. Ria, bring Kaja through to the office will you?'

They came into the office and Ria gestured for Kaja to sit on the small sofa, which I'd bought it out of my own wallet, I might add.

'Kaja, I won't ask you how you're feeling. It goes without saying.' The lass had the face of a little girl lost. 'Have you heard anything from Reeta?' My thoughts were already expecting a negative response, which was confirmed when she shook her head. Seeing as the introductions had already been made, I got straight to the point, and for the next forty-five minutes I had Kaja repeat her story.

'What will happen now?' The girl asked.

'You just leave it to us. Try not to worry too much.' I tried to sound optimistic. To be truthful, I doubted my own words. I can, in all honesty, say in nine times out of ten situations like this we do find the missing girls, just not always alive. 'Won't be a minute,' I said to the girl and nodded to Ria, and then towards the squad room. 'I don't know about you but I reckon we should pay that place a visit. What do you reckon?' I said once the door was closed behind us.

'Can't lose anything can we, but what about the vice lads?'

'Bugger vice, this is our case. Let's get back in.'

'Treading a fine line, "H",' Ria said as she opened the office door and went back in shaking her head.

'Kaja, I don't think it's a very good idea you going back to the house, do you?

'I have to…Reeta, she might come back?'

'I've said, we will do everything we can to find your sister, but, I'm sure you will agree we have to stop these people doing it to other girls?' There was just the slightest of nods in agreement. 'Good.'

'Have you anywhere else you can stay?' Ria asked Kaja.

She shook her head. 'No, nowhere.'

'Don't worry, we can sort something out for you,' Ria reassured the girl.

'First things first,' I said. 'Can you get back to the house and pack a bag without drawing any attention to yourself? You know, without being seen?'

Kaja said it was possible, as Alexei left the house around twelve o'clock for an hour to go to the pub for his lunch. Ria told her to grab whatever belongings she could easily carry and agreed to pick her up at the corner of Hessle Road and Coltman Street at 12.45 p.m. I emphasised how important it was that she told no-one where she'd been, or what was going on, as I was planning to raid the house. I had one more thing to do before I left my office, set the wheels in motion to see if we could find Reeta, I made the call to the regional Vice Squad, omitting to mention our pending operation.

***

Bang on 12.45 p.m. as Ria pulled the car into the kerb edge, Kaja glanced over her shoulder and promptly opened the back door and climbed in. Five minutes later we were all sat in my office again as Kaja gave us a rundown on the layout of the house. The next thing we had to do was sort out hostel accommodation for Kaja, although Ria wasn't convinced a hostel was the best solution, because it was easily traceable. I could see where she was coming from, especially from the security aspect. We reckoned that maybe a women's refuge might be safer. I left Ria to sort out the details, and parked the girl, with another mug of coffee, at one of the spare desks in the squad room while the arrangements were made.
***

When Questy and Samantha got back from a wasted trip to Selby, I called the team together for a briefing and opted to make our raid early morning around 2 a.m. I reckoned at that time of the morning, the place would still be open for business and we should catch them with their pants down, so to speak. It was unfortunate we'd knock up the overtime bill, but what the hell, the team wouldn't mind.

By my reckoning they must have put Kaja on the missing list by now. Seeing as though the canteen was closed for the night except for brewing up, it was pizzas all round for CID. Uniform could look after themselves. Hard, I know, but I'm not made of money and it was coming out of my own pocket.

The overtime had started to mount up, I dreaded to think how the Super was going to take it, probably send me the bill if we didn't get a result. The canteen was full of light-hearted banter, then quietened down as the night went on. In line with procedure I'd held a briefing, telling the individual teams what was expected. Midnight came and went and everyone was itching to get on with it. By the time it reached 2 a.m., we were parked up within easy access to our target address. Myself, Ria, Questy and DC Steve Wales were in the lead car: Steve's not only a half decent detective, he's one of these weight lifting, rugby playing types, a good bloke to watch your back in difficult situations. I wouldn't be without him, a handy lad in a tussle.

Samantha was in car two, along with three DCs. I'd told her, due to the lack of experience in these sort of things, she was to hang back and wait while we were all inside, but she didn't like it one bit. The heavy gang of the uniform Task Force, along with a couple of female officers, waited in an unmarked van down the tenfoot a half a dozen houses away. And we had a team of uniforms covering the back exit.

The three storey terraced house was mid-way down Coltman Street, about 150 metres from Hessle Road. Considering the area and what the premises were used for, the house looked to be in pretty good nick, UPVC windows and door, tidy looking blinds up at the windows and the main door opened straight onto the street. From what the Kaja had told us, there were three rooms and a kitchen on the ground floor, two were divided off to resemble massage treatment rooms, and there was also a basement room which belonged to Alexei. On the first floor were four bedrooms, a bathroom and a third floor attic room, which was always kept locked, the girls weren't allowed anywhere near it. The attic was the initiation room for the new girls, and according to Kaja, it was occupied.

The sleet was building up on the windscreen and the car blower was making hard work of clearing the condensation off. Steve Wales kept putting the wipers on, wipers off, wipers on. It didn't do a lot of good, all it did was irritate me.

'Give it up, Steve.' The bugger was getting on my nerves, he was tapping his fingers on the steering wheel in between flicking the wiper switch.

'Sorry, Boss. I hate all this waiting.'

'Won't be long now,' I told him.

We didn't know if the house was fully occupied with punters and if so how many there might be. Kaja said all the girls would be present and at the most, one minder along with this Alexei. By my reckoning we had only seen a couple of punters come and go. Someone was going to have to do some serious explaining to their spouses at some point in the very near future. Not my problem, nothing more than they deserved.

Patience is always a virtue on these operations, a virtue Steve didn't have. I picked up my AirWaves handset and pressed the push-to-talk button. 'Everyone keep your places, DO NOT COCK THIS UP!' I reminded them. Punters came and punters went as they say, all the while we watched until I felt the time was right. From Kaja's description, the muscle who kept letting the punters in must be been Alexei. He looked to be around six feet tall, a big lad with muscles stretching his T-shirt and arms that, due to the muscle, couldn't hang straight by his side; I reckon he'd be a match for Steve Wales any day of the week.

The plan was simple: I was going to pretend to be a punter and walk straight up to the door and knock. With any luck I'd be let in, then, as I entered, the cavalry would get a spurt on and follow me through the door. That was the plan anyway. On the negative side, just in case things didn't pan out the way I'd planned, one of the lads would be ready with the steel enforcer just in case the door was slammed in my face. Uniform would have the back way covered to stop anybody trying to make a run for it.

It was time. 'Listen up,' I said into the AirWaves, 'as soon as you see the door open, move. Don't leave me stood there like a prick.' I put the radio in my pocket. 'Right, Mike,' I said. 'Time to move,' I opened the car door and got out; it was cold enough to freeze your balls off. I stuck my head back through the open car window. 'Don't let them cock this up, please,' I almost begged Questy.

I pulled my jacket collar up, tucked my head in and walked up the pavement, all casual with a slight sway as if I'd had a few, I could see a CCTV camera above the front door monitoring whoever approached. I stopped in front of the white UPVC door and knocked, I didn't have to wait long.

'Can I help you?' The bruiser said in broken English through the slightly open door. I could see that the safety chain was on.

'Alright pal,' I said smiling and swaying, still acting a bit pissed. 'This the place, right? I mean, know what I mean, jiggy-jiggy?' Still smiling, I gave him a wink and patted my jacket pocket where my wallet was. He nodded and opened the door fully.

I heard the team pounding the pavement behind me. Wham! I moved forward, slamming my right shoulder into the door; it bounced back at me at the speed of light, knocking me off balance. All to the good, I heaved myself forward again, my left shoulder caught the doorman in the middle of his chest. Winded, he fell backwards and I bounced off him on to the floor like a sack of spuds. The next thing, Questy, Steve and Ria pushed past me along with the rest of the team and disappeared all over the house, shouting, "Police!" as they went. Samantha was last to enter, she was wearing a skirt; I screwed my eyes tight closed as she stepped over my face.

One of the uniforms was kneeling none too gently in the middle of Alexei's back, stretching his muscular arms around the back and putting the cuffs on. I scrambled to my feet, puffing and panting, and followed the team down the hall. I could hear the lads shouting out warnings as they tramped about upstairs. Things were going to plan, for a change. As Kaja had told us, besides Alexei's room in the basement, there was a kitchen and three other rooms downstairs divided into "treatment" cubicles; magnolia emulsion had been slapped on the walls and plasterboard partitions, but they stank. Despite the obvious attempt to freshen them with cheap air freshener, the scabby rooms smelled of stale male sweat and sex.

Girls were screaming as they tried to cover themselves, and punters panicking trying to pull their trousers on as the uniforms rounded them all up. The staircase leading to the upper floors was in the hallway directly opposite the front door, and was where the girls' living accommodation was. Once I got my breath back I bounded up the stairs to the girls' bedrooms: each room had two single beds and minimal crappy second-hand furniture. They were a bit better than the rooms downstairs, ok I was lying, and they were bloody manky. I could see that on the whole, the girls had tried to make the best of a bad situation, by trying to brighten the rooms up with photographs and posters over the peeling wallpaper.

Further along the upstairs hall was an even narrower staircase covered in a threadbare carpet which led to the attic. I took the stairs two at a time, Ria followed. There was only one room at the top and it was locked; a big steel padlock secured the room.

'Steve,' I yelled down the stairs. 'Get the bolt cutters from the car and don't fuck about.'

'Oh shit,' Ria said over my shoulder, she'd read my thoughts.

I was dreading going into the room. Steve thundered up the stairs two at a time and pushed us aside. He fixed the jaws of the cutters firmly on the steel hasp of the lock and squeezed the handle, the veins on the back of his hands looked as if they were going to pop, CRACK! The steel snapped and the lock fell to the floor. He moved to one side to let us pass.

Afraid of what I was about to see, I cautiously pushed the door open with my foot. The stench was overpowering, horrendous, I put my hand up to cover my mouth. A single dim light bulb hung from a flex in the ceiling, it barely lit the room. The only natural light would have come from a frost covered filthy glass panel in the sloping roof. A disgustingly filthy single bed sized mattress stood against the damp wall opposite where I stood. I caught my breath as I went further into the room; an ancient single bed with a stained mattress, covered by a thin sheet was the only furniture, discounting the piss bucket on the floor beside it. On the bed lay a frightened girl, curling herself into a ball as if trying to make herself invisible. She couldn't have been any older than sixteen. My stomach did somersaults as I looked at her.

I was struck dumb and ashamed to say I was rooted to the spot for a second or two. Ria gave me a shove and took the lead, she was already kneeling by the bedside by the time I'd pulled myself together. She was talking softly to the girl, who lay cowering, afraid. Dirty underwear was all the girl was wearing, her skin was a pallid grey colour, she must have been freezing. Then I saw the manacle and chain around her ankle, it was just long enough to allow her to use the stinking bucket.

'For fuck's sake, Steve, bring those bolt cutters. Samantha, find a blanket,' I kept my voice low, she was frightened enough. Steve cut the chain and then took off his jacket and laid it over the girl. I was already on the AirWaves calling for an ambulance. All the time this was happening, Ria stayed by the girl's side with a comforting arm around her.

I stood back and left the girl to Ria, she's better at these sort of things than me. From what I could make out, the girl didn't speak any English. She just kept mumbling as Ria tried to comfort her.

I bounded downstairs. Questy had put Alexei in the kitchen, which was as much of a dump as the rest of the place, polluted. The door minder sat on a kitchen chair with his handcuffed hands resting in his lap. He looked up with a smug smile on his face. I had a quick glance around over my shoulder, there was only Questy. The fingers of my right hand were already curling in and out of a tight fist, I drew my arm back and gave the shit such a fucking thump on the side of his head, he fell to the floor. I thought I'd broken my hand. At least he wasn't looking smug any more.

'Bastard,' I said.

'Never saw a thing,' Questy said as he turned away from me, Alexei was on his knees nursing his head with his cuffed hands.

'Where have you put the punters?' I was rubbing my knuckles, I could feel my hand swelling up.

'In one of the treatment cubicles, they're all moaning like hell.'

'How many of them?'

'Six.'

'Don't mess about, have them all taken down the nick and let them stew a while before they are cautioned, get their statements and frighten them to fucking death.'

'Right you lot, get your pants on.'

'Bugger that, they can go as they are!' As six punters were being led away in their underpants I had a thought. 'Put them in the cells for the rest of the night, teach the bastards to keep their brains in their trousers. In the morning, have uniform do a follow-up, I want it let slip to their other halves what they've been up to.'

Unethical I know, but these sods were their own worst enemies, responsible for their own actions and, more importantly, accountable for the poor girl waiting for the ambulance. The other girls had been put in the front bedroom; they all looked frightened as I walked in, still rubbing my knuckles. 'Do any of them speak English?' I asked Samantha.

'Not a word, Si—Boss, they all reckon they can't understand,' she said. I gave her one of those raised eyebrow looks.

I was hoping at least one of them would be able to speak English, but if they could, they were keeping quiet about it. I was hopeful to get one of them to act as an interpreter for the girl upstairs—no chance of that: they were all too frightened. It wasn't long before the ambulance turned up with its blues and twos blaring out. The paramedics wrapped the girl in a thermal blanket, put her in a small wheelchair and carried her down the stairs and into the ambulance. I turned to Questy. 'Do you know if there are any Crime Scene people on the night shift?'

'You must be joking, Harry: nine 'til five, that lot.'

'Ok, have a quick look around and then have uniform secure the house, I want someone outside all night. You never know, Tosh and his lot might find something useful'. Tosh was our resident Chief Crime Scene Examiner, good bloke, Lard Arse we call him behind his back on account of him having, yes you've guessed, a large arse. 'Try some sign language and get the girls to pack a small bag each, call for a couple of cars and take them down to the station. Make sure they're all ok and I'll meet you back at the nick.' I walked out of the kitchen.

'Another one, sir,' a uniformed officer called as I was about to go out of the front door. I turned around to see what was going on. Two uniforms came marching up the hallway dragging another bloke cuffed between them. He was a good five feet ten inches tall, with muscle that looked like it had gone to seed a bit.

'Punter?' I asked.

'No sir, he reckons he's a twenty-four hour plumber come to sort out the bathroom tap.'

'Plumber my arse!'

'As soon as we came through the back door, he sneaked out of that walk-in cupboard and tried to get around the back of us.'

'You English?' He didn't answer, I walked close up. 'Do you speak English?' I was right in his face, his breath smelled of booze. 'Sod it, I've had enough for one night, arrest him and take him away with the other fucker, and keep them separate.'

I went out to the car, sat in the driving seat and had a smoke, then drove back to the nick.

Chapter 7
The Policeman Tries To Remember

'Ria, you are a life saver,' I said as she brought me a steaming mug. 'What a night. Heard anything from the hospital yet?'

'Samantha's down there now, said she'll let us know as soon as she hears anything.'

'What about an interpreter?' I sat back and rubbed my knuckles. 'Ouch.' My fingers and the back of my hand had started to turn a yellowy purple colour. My hand was twice its usual size.

'Nobody to blame but yourself, "H", it serves you right. You know better than to assault a prisoner.' No sympathy there, then.

'Who said I assaulted anybody?' Questy has a big gob.

'You should go and have it X-rayed.'

'Later maybe. Interpreter?' I tried flexing my fingers, I think Ria might be right about an X-ray.

'We can't get hold of one until the morning.'

I pushed back my chair, partly pulled out one of the desk drawers, sat back with my feet resting on the drawer edge and held my mug with my good hand.

'What do reckon we should do about the girls? Are we keeping them here all night?' Ria asked me.

'What other option is there? Unless you want to take them home with you for a sleep over? On the face of it, they're here working illegally: no matter what the situation is, we've no other choice than to process them.'

'Leave it to Samantha then?'

'That's what she's here for; suppose they'll all end up being deported. Just make sure they're all comfortable for the rest of the night.'

Ria looked half asleep herself, Questy was looking a bit too comfortable on the sofa. I finished the brew and kicked the drawer shut, making Mike open his eyes. 'Tell you what, sort the girls and let's call it a day, or night, or whatever, and sort it out in the morning.' I was knackered. I didn't bother tidying my desk, I headed off home.

***

I knew it was late in the evening—or early in the morning depending on how you looked at it—but a dram or two was called for just to calm the nerves. Bugger the doctor, this was my ideal way of relaxing, lounging in my big comfy chair and watching the small world of the marina through the glass doors. On a summer evening, I would sit with the patio doors wide open until the small hours and it was time for bed: more often than not, it would be until I woke up. I nodded off more since my attack. I liked dark winter nights like these, the eerie sight of the marina covered in a light snow and glistening frost, shimmering in the glow of lights.

Wow, that was almost poetic, for me. I sat and watched the—well, nothing really— just the uncontaminated winter nightscape. Looking out over the boats, I tried to think back to the night of my heart attack. I'd had a good evening meal out at a Greek restaurant with Questy and his partner William, and then a taxi back to the marina, so far so good. I remember walking along the quayside; this is the bit I can't work out, see if you can. Feeling content and thinking how good life was, I ambled along minding my own business. I could see this bloke lurking in the shadows, but then again that's nothing strange for this neck of the woods. Now this *was* surreal, I remember that I started to whistle. I can't for the life of me ever, ever, remember whistling in my entire life. The more I whistled, the more the bloke in the shadows seemed to get nearer and nearer, I could almost see his face, then... you know the rest.

At the hospital, they told me if the girl hadn't carried out CPR until the ambulance arrived, I'd have been a goner. It wasn't too long before my eyes started closing, sure enough, I headed off to bed and slept with the smell of her perfume in my head and dreamed.

I barely seemed to be in bed any time when the alarm clock took over. "It's half past six, it's time to get up, it's half past six, it's time to get up," the thing was yelling at me. Clumsily I reached out to turn it off, wishing I'd never bought the noisy bloody thing. I just wanted to put my head under the duvet and get back to my dream. Dreams? Questions unanswered? Incomplete thoughts? I don't know what they were, but something in the back of my mind kept trying to push itself to the forefront.

Sitting at the kitchen table with a slice of toast and mug of tea, I tried to make sense of it. Ok, I know it was only a dream, but they say there is an element of truth in them, don't they? What's that word when you get that feeling you've been somewhere before? Déjà vu? Could it be? I was buggered if I knew. There was only one thing for it, so I headed off for a shower and got myself ready for work.

***

After spending ten minutes of slipping, sliding and scraping ice off the car windscreen, I was finally able to drive into the office. Surprisingly, after such a late night, most of the team were in before me.

'Mike, how's it going? We haven't had a chance to catch up.'

'Not much to tell, Harry.'

'All the same, grab a hold of Samantha and you can fill me in on what's happening.' He gave me a funny look. 'Well you would have done one time.' He did that thing he always does, touching his hair on the back of his shirt collar; a subconscious thing he does when he's caught off guard. 'Give me a few minutes, then come through, and bring a brew with you.' I smiled to myself. I looked around the squad room, Ria was just coming in loaded up with files, she edged in backwards trying to push open the door with her arse. 'Meeting in my office when you're sorted,' I said.

'Can you just get the door pl…' she called out.

I smiled to myself again and pretended I hadn't heard her. I did hear her call me a twat, though. Sat behind my desk, I switched the computer on. Bloody emails, my inbox was full of them. I did what I usually do, ignored them, even the ones promising to enlarge my manhood.

Mike and Samantha duly arrived, followed by a grumpy looking DS Middleton.

'Thanks, Mike.' He put the brew down on my desk. Samantha brought her own and the biscuits.

Ria was next, and you should have seen the filthy look she gave Questy as he put my mug down. She looked at him and then at the mugs and back.

'I didn't realise you were in on this, sorry.' Questy said.

To say a little tension had developed between Mike and Ria since Samantha had joined the team would be an understatement. Surely Ria didn't fancy her? I couldn't be doing with another Questy situation.

'Done any good with the interpreter?'

'Same as yesterday, seems the university are running on skeleton staff with it being the winter break.'

'Bloody hell, it's alright for bloody academics, but it's not a lot of good to us.'

Ria was quick to respond. 'I'm going to contact the council when we've finished, see if we can get any joy there.'

Then I had a thought.

'Get in touch with the women's refuge, have Steve Wales pick Kaja up and take her to the Infirmary. Then she can come back to the nick and try to explain things to the girls in custody.'

'Is she the same nationality?' Samantha asked me.

'Buggered if I know, sounds near enough to me.' I could see Ria shaking her head at my stereotyping, but I was desperate. 'Anyone heard how the girl is?'

'In hospital speak, "comfortable", if that means anything to you?' Ria was quick off the mark again, a little competition never did any harm.

'Not a lot, what sort of statement is comfortable? Anyone would think the girl was sat on a bloody sofa watching the telly. Samantha, why don't you tag along with Mike and see what Tosh and his lot are up to?'

'Tag along? You don't have to patronise me, Harry.' Wow, I didn't bank on having to cope with this verbal sparring.

'I wasn't aware that I was, just that you're still getting to know how the team operates. It's not quite the same as working Customs and Immigration but you're getting there.'

'But—'

I cut her off. 'Not quite time to go solo yet.' Oh dear, I'd upset her, but I could live with that. Samantha edged Questy out of the way and made for the door. 'Hang on,' I said, 'When you've done that, I want a property search done with the Land Agency. Is the house rented? Who owns it? That sort of thing.' Questy nodded and Samantha flicked her hair. 'Are we having another brew?' I asked Ria.

'What about interviewing the two blokes from last night?'

'Leave them stewing for a while. Are we having that brew or what?' As usual she tutted and shook her head, then unusually for Ria, she shouted the full length of the squad room for Russ to get the drinks. 'And bring me a bacon sarnie,' I yelled through the open door. She stuck her head back around the door and gave me a '*should you be having that?*' type of look. 'Before you say anything I'm bloody fed up with muesli, ok? And don't forget the ketchup.' All I got was another shake of the head and tut as the door closed behind her.

***

After I'd fed my face, I decided it was time to see if we could get anything out of the two tosspots we'd brought in previous evening. Interview room two was definitely not the one I'd have chosen. For some reason unknown to me, or anybody else for that matter, it always smelled manky. Like dodgy drains at the best of times. The added smell of stale sweat and vodka coming from the scrote sat at the other side of the table didn't help. I pitied the poor uniform sat in the corner keeping an eye on the Russian.

Alexei had a lovely lump and a black and purple bruise on the left side of his head, just below his shaven hairline. I had my own reminder of the previous night, a fat fist. I flinched as I automatically clenched my fingers. The Russian didn't acknowledge we'd entered the room, just sat there bulging out of his T-shirt. I sat there staring the bugger straight in the face, my DS beside me. Ria set the tape machine going, and for the benefit of the tape, stated the time and who was in the room, then read him his rights. The video camera fixed in the top corner of the room was in action, keeping an eye on things to make sure I didn't crack him again. I asked him if he wanted a lawyer. He didn't say a word, but with his silent contempt it was taken that he'd refused legal representation. This wasn't going to be easy.

'You understand why you're here?' I asked the Russian.

'Yah nee pah nee MAH yoo.'

'Would you please speak English?' I was being very civil, all considered.

'Yah nee pah nee MAH yoo.' He shook his head.

'And what does that mean when it's at home? Are you telling me you don't speak English?' He just smiled, so I guess I was right. I was well and truly pissed off and looked towards Ria to take over.

'Please state your full name, nationality and address,' she asked him. She got the same silent contempt as I had. The slimy sod just sat there with a cheesy grin on his face.

'You bloody well understood what I was saying last night when you were arrested,' I shouted as I slammed the flats of my hands down on the table. This was getting us nowhere and we still had the other one to have a go at. I stood up, nearly pushing the tubular chair over and stormed out of the room, leaving Ria to terminate the interview.

Wanker.

I went out for a nicotine fix.

By the time I'd calmed myself down and gone back in the building, sucking on an extra strong mint, my hand was really starting to give me some gyp and throbbing like buggery. I decided I'd better go and have it X-rayed when I got chance. Ria had prat number two ready and waiting in the interview room, but I wasn't holding my breath.

I walked in, dropped the folder I was carrying onto the table and sat down. I didn't make eye contact. I made myself comfortable, put my specs on, opened the folder and with the occasional tut and shake of the head I made a convincing show of pretending to read it.

Ria knew my routine and set the tape machine running, made the introductions stating who was in the room, informed our prisoner of his legal rights and then duly charged him.

This time we were more successful. At least he could speak English, just. I say English... he was from Glasgow. His name was Allan Roose, not the best looking bloke in the world or even Hull for that matter. With his round, fat face and over-hanging eye lids, it seemed as if his left eye was looking for his right, but his several times broken nose was in the way. He looked as if he should have been called Moose, never mind Roose. All told he was an ugly bastard, the type of face only a mother could have loved, I think.

Steve Wales had run Moose's—sorry, a Freudian slip—Roose's, details through the PNC. He had a charge sheet as long as my arm: GBH, aggravated assault, possession with intent to supply, the list went on and a quick glance was all I needed.

'Bloody hell, Allan, you *have* been a busy lad.' He smiled through crooked teeth. 'You have the right to a solicitor, if you don't have one we can appoint one for you.' I reminded him. He just sat there like a lemon.

'Do you want a brief, or not?' Ria asked him.

'I know the procedure and I can'a see any point just yet.' He spoke in a broad Glaswegian accent. I had to really strain to make out what he was saying.

'The choice is yours, Allan, but you will need one at some stage.'

'Aye I know, maybe in a wee while.'

He knew he was in deep shit. He said he'd been living in Hull for the past three months, doing a bit of this and that. I didn't have time to ask him to elaborate, I had a feeling it would have taken the rest of the day. He was just a soldier, muscle hired to help if any of the customers started to rough up the girls. He said he knew bugger all about the girl in the attic, nor how the operation functioned, and I believed him. It turned out Roose and Alexei were casual drinking buddies, had the odd game of darts etc and he jumped at the chance of some easy money. All he had to do was work the door and give the occasional punter a slap. Cash in hand. Easy money. Simples.

'Mr Roose, do you know anything about the girls being sent out to private parties?'

'Happens.'

'Do you have an address?'

'Sorry can't help you there, I only work the door, remember? They don't tell me stuff like that.'

'One more question, we're led to believe auctions are held at these parties, girls sold to the highest bidder, can you throw any light on this?'

'Aye, well, as far as I know it's not an auction. Some Newcastle mob has first refusal on the tarts, that's all I know.'

The interview was duly terminated. 'At least now we've got an inkling as to where Kaja's sister might be,' I said when we were back out in the corridor. 'Give Northumbria Police in Newcastle a call will you?' *Good news?* Maybe.

***

The Hull Infirmary car park was, as usual, overflowing. I was in half a mind to park on the double yellow lines. Some time ago, I'd parked in a restricted area and had to spend twenty minutes scraping a day-glow "no parking" sticker off the windscreen. I pulled up and stopped.

'Well,' I said to Ria, 'where would you park?' She pointed towards a vacant 'doctors only' space, I pulled in and she put a *Police* sticker in the windscreen.

We trudged through the ankle-high slush of the car park, and went in through the front entrance of the 1960s tower block. The Infirmary was undergoing a vast refurbishment but you couldn't tell that from the outside; at least the scaffolding that seemed as if it had been up for years, holding the tile façade, had been removed. The entrance to the foyer was chock full of smokers crowding the entrance, and this was just the patients, some even in their pyjamas and wheel-chairs, connected up to mobile drips, and it was bloody freezing.

Hospitals, I hated the bloody places. Even though the staff at the Castle Hill Hospital had recently saved my life, I couldn't help the way I feel.

According to a frumpy woman behind the reception desk, our girl was in a private room on the fourth floor. Heave up, heave down again, that was how my stomach felt as the lift moved upwards at the speed of light, then whoa! The lift abruptly stopped, my stomach did a somersault as it fell to my boots, it took me all my time not throw up. All Ria did was smirk.

A uniform on sentry duty sat outside the girl's door reading the *Sun,* I use the term sentry very loosely.

'Oi!' I shouted. He nearly fell off the bloody chair 'Doing the crossword?' I gave him an *'I'll remember you'* type of look and we went in. He muttered something I was probably glad I didn't hear. Steve opened the door to see what the commotion was.

'Everything ok, Boss?'

I threw a backwards glance to the uniform outside and walked into the room.

'Harry, it is good to see you.' Kaja said as she stood up from her chair.

'And you too.' She looked well, very well, came closer and reached up and kissed me on the cheek, her perfume... Bloody hell, that perfume! I remembered where I'd come across it before. The thoughts were whizzing back and forth in my head until I felt dizzy; to stop myself from dropping to the floor I clung to her a bit too long, drinking in the fragrance. There was no way this performance wouldn't go unnoticed by my colleagues and I was right. Ria gave me a sly smile, and cheeky bugger Steve Wales even dared give me a wink; no doubt he would be telling everybody when we got back to the station.

'Is everything ok at the refuge?' Like a teenager on a first date, I struggled to get the words out.

'Yes, ok, thank you, Harry.' She didn't sound very convincing.

To distance myself from Kaja for a second or two, I turned to face Steve. 'How's she doing?' I nodded towards the girl snuggled in her bed.

'Not so bad Boss, according to the doctor she just needs plenty of rest and feeding up a bit.'

'What about the drugs?'

'They're keeping a close watch and giving her Methadone to help the withdrawal, the doctor said they'll get her onto a rehab programme as soon as she's well enough.'

'Not had a word with the girl then?'

'No Boss, thought it best to wait 'til you got here.'

I motioned Kaja to the edge of the bed, I didn't want to crowd the girl out and stayed back against the wall, Kaja relayed my questions to the girl. As luck would have it, language wasn't a barrier—she was from the Ukraine, same as Kaja.   It turned out the poor little bugger was only fifteen, her name was Bohdana Chuzhoi. It was the same old story, she was an only child, the mother was dead and she lived with her old man. The father was up to his neck in debt to a nasty piece of work, a debt he didn't have a cat in hell's chance of paying off. So her father, if you can call him that, was offered a solution to all his problems, which was to sell Bohdana into prostitution.

For the previous three months before she ended up in the UK, she had lived and worked in a brothel on an industrial estate on the outskirts of Kiev in the Ukraine. The brothel went under the guise of being called the International Hotel, mainly frequented by truckers from right across Europe. Like many other girls who had been lured or sold into the profession, she had been kept locked up 24/7, she and fifteen other girls had been used and abused by all and sundry from morning 'til night in a never-ending cycle. She remembered being dragged from her bed in the early hours of the morning, she wasn't given any time to gather her meagre belongings together before a needle was shoved into her arm. Half carried and half dragged, she remembered being bundled into the back of a lorry, then she passed out. She didn't remember anything about the people or the journey, just waking up frightened to death to find herself manacled to the bed in the manky attic room. Poor cow didn't even know how long she'd been there, she never left the room; every time she woke up, someone was always there ready with another needle. Food was a luxury between fixes.

We'd gleaned as much information as we could, unfortunately there was very little that could help the immediate investigation at hand. 'Kaja,' I said as the others walked ahead. 'I think we need to have a talk, don't we? Come around to the apartment tonight, ok?' She dipped her head in small sullen nods.

Best get my hand checked out, I'd decided, so I looked at the overhead signs and made my way to Accident and Emergency. An hour and a bloody half I was stuck in that place, only to be told it was badly bruised. "Take some paracetamols" the Doc told me—I had something a bit better at the apartment. Anyway, with a strapped-up hand that was twice its usual size and throbbing like buggery, I phoned the nick and then headed off home.

***

Later that evening, Kaja and I sat in my lounge with a couple of glasses of wine, putting off the inevitable for as long as possible. After a while of making small talk, Kaja stood and walked across to the French doors and looked out across the marina.

'That night when I brought you back to the apartment, why didn't you tell me it was you who found me?' I asked.

'Because I am ashamed.' She still had her back to me; I could see her reflection in the glass looking as she stared out at the water.

'Ashamed of what, saving my life?' I was puzzled by her answer.

'No, I am ashamed because I stole from you.' Wow, this surprised me.

'When?' I was stumped for words.

'The night you had heart attack, before ambulance came I took money from your wallet.'

I didn't have a clue any money had been nicked. 'How much?' I asked.

'Twenty pounds,' she said sheepishly with her head down looking at the floor. 'I was so ashamed, it was hard for me to tell you after you were kind to me.'

Twenty pounds. Well I laughed so hard I nearly pissed myself, as they say. I would have given this girl all the money I had for saving my life. The girl wondered why I'd laughed so much, she thought I'd be angry, but who could be angry, twenty quid in exchange for my life? No contest.

'I had been working and saw you fall, I thought you were drunk, and when you did not get up I went to see if I could help. I called for ambulance, your coat was opened wide, I stole the money. When ambulance came, I left.'

'Did you see anyone else there or hear anyone?'

'No, no-one, only you, no-one else.' Strange.

'Now we've got that sorted, you'll be pleased to know we've got a lead as to where Reeta might have been taken.' The girl's face was a picture, a smile a mile long that soon turned to tear-filled eyes.

'You have found her?'

'Not exactly, we think she may have been taken to work in Newcastle.'

'Where is Newcastle?'

'Further north, a city on the east coast. We've already been in contact with the police up there and they're doing all they can to find Reeta.'

The next thing I knew she was up out of her seat and throwing her arms around me and giving me a bear hug. 'Thank you Harry, thank you.'

Chapter 8
The Gangster Returns

There was no doubt in my mind, Newcastle is a great city. There was nothing pressing waiting for me back in Hull, so after dropping Reeta and the other girl off at their new "home", I thought I'd take advantage of the Geordie hospitality for a couple of days.

The guy I was doing business with is a big wheel in the city, night clubs, taxis and girls, you know the sort of thing. My new friend is also the part owner of the city centre hotel where I was going to relax for a couple of days. Talk about posh, the place was well fitted out. I stood and looked around the reception area, very nice. I put on my best smile and walked over to reception, the snotty bloke behind the desk gave me a look like I'd stepped in dog shit. I gave him the Michael Caine snake-eye look and his attitude soon changed when I told him who sent me. 'No problem, sir,' he said to me; all smiles, the phoney bastard.

I spent a few pleasant hours in the hotel; my new friend had laid on some nice female company for *gratis*, two of them. It was a pleasant surprise as I wasn't expecting to hang around—the next day I had to do a bit of shopping for essentials and then settled myself in the bar with a pint of Newcastle Brown, I was really looking forward to see what the coming evening had in store. Then the mobile rang, I rejected the call, but whoever it was, persisted. They weren't giving up. I should have picked it up first time.

It was a message from one of my colleagues back in Hull; the girl I'd had a go at and thrown out into the snow had done a runner. That was all I fucking needed, some jumped-up slapper on walkabout. I made a couple of calls and set the wheels in motion to try to find the slag. I wanted her back. Who the fuck did she think she was?

As if that wasn't enough, the icing on the cake was that the house down Coltman Street had been raided, and that wasn't going to go down well with the boss, especially since we had a new girl in the attic, breaking her in. This meant serious trouble; what's more, it meant money down the drain. So much for a couple of days' R and R. I packed up what belongings I'd bought, said my goodbyes, got back in the BMW and clogged it back down the A1.

***

I arrived back in the city around about tea time; over a pint and a whisky chaser I put the word out among the streets' low-lifes that a crisp £50 note and a nice little bag of coke was waiting for whoever found my girl.

I thought I'd better have a look-see what was going on with the house, so I took a drive into Coltman Street. Came in from the Anlaby Road end and drove straight past our premises then parked up with a clear view in the rear view mirror. It looked like the police hadn't finished with it, several lengths of that blue and white plastic tape they use was fixed across the door. Sod it, there was bugger all I could do. I made a couple of calls and I wasn't surprised to find out that Alexei had been remanded in custody. I didn't reckon he'd have any chance of bail. Maybe if we hadn't had the girl in the attic he might have got away with it, but hey-ho, that's life. Then my mobile rang. Bloody things were going from bad to worse; at one of our other premises back in the city an over-enthusiastic punter had accidentally topped one of the girls.

Shit.

I told Gerry; he's the bloke that rang me. "Give the punter a fucking good hiding, get his debit card, credit cards and clean the fucker out." Even though she wasn't one of our top earners, there was no way we were going to be out of pocket on this. If I had to go back and make the twat sign his house over I would, I'd done it before. As for the dead girl, I told him, just get rid. Then I had a thought and gave him a call back: 'Shove her in the freezer.'

Chapter 9
The Policeman's Nightmare'

Things were happening a bit too slowly for my liking. Tosh, our Senior Crime Scene Examiner and his team, were in it up to their necks at the house. He said there was a good week's work to be done and that was just on the attic room. Tosh reckoned with the number of fingerprints and DNA samples that needed taking for elimination, it would take until next Christmas for the results to come back. Hopefully not. We'd managed to get hold of an interpreter, so were able to start the interviews with the girls. They were as much in the dark as us as to who was running the operation. Either that, or they were too frightened to say for fear of repercussions to their families back home. Uniform was carrying out door to door enquiries down Coltman Street, so all in all it was a waiting game to see what came to light. All the same, I wasn't holding my breath.

All the time this was going on, we still had the bread and butter work to contend with, assaults, breaking and entering and so forth, but for CID this wasn't anything we couldn't cope with. Mike and Samantha were following up with the Land Registry, and at the same time following a paper trail concerning the driver of the lorry that brought the drugs in from Rotterdam. I decided I should take advantage of the temporary lull and start to make headway through the paperwork that had started to mount up. That was what was supposed to happen, but I'd been letting things get on top of me and I was in one of those unsociable moods and needed to be out of the office for a while. Ria was holding the fort in the office, so I made a break for it and skived off for an hour or so.

I drove out to the McDonalds' drive through on St. Andrew's Quay, I know I shouldn't eat the stuff, but if people didn't know they couldn't rollock me. With my brown paper bag of fries and double cheeseburger on the seat beside me, I'd driven across and parked up near the safety rail looking out over the River Humber. Staring through the windscreen at the seagulls hovering over the murky Humber, I didn't feel too good, butterflies in my stomach. I couldn't blame the burger, it was still in the bag. I had that awful feeling again.

Out of the blue I was feeling really ill. I'd broken out in a cold sweat, my stomach decided to do somersaults and my chest began to flutter and heave as I struggled to catch my breath. Oh hell, this was it! I thought I was having another heart attack, the curtain's coming down for the final time.

I seemed to be stuck to the seat and my arms hung by my side, paralysed. I started to panic and tried to reach for my mobile but my hands wouldn't work. Jesus, what was happening to me? Sitting facing the windscreen I could see a shape forming in the condensation, no, not a shape—a face materialising out of nowhere. Oh shit, the face was staring and grinning at me. Condensation began dripping down the windscreen, the face turned into rivulets and ran down the glass. My eyes closed.

Eventually my eyes opened. It was only condensation. How long had I been asleep, two minutes, five minutes? I didn't know, my watch had stopped; when I checked the dashboard clock it was flashing on and off. *'Breaths, deep breaths,'* I told myself, keeping calm as my eyes closed and opened. The dashboard clock was working again, my watch was working—seconds, only seconds had passed since I'd parked up, oh shit.

I opened the door and vomited onto the tarmac. I closed the door and wiped my mouth on the back of my sleeve, opened the car window and fed my burger and fries to the seagulls.

My breathing had eventually steadied, I was back to normal and I flipped the top off my coffee, sipped, thinking maybe the caffeine fix would help. It didn't. I took out my cigarettes and studied the packet for a moment or two. Should I? Shouldn't I? I knew it wouldn't do me good. I crushed the cigarette in my hand and threw it out of the car, to be devoured by the gulls. There was no way I was going back to the nick. I rang the office and gave Ria a sob story about not feeling too good, well it was the truth in some respect, I wasn't going to tell her I thought I was cracking up. Very, very carefully I drove home, feeling like a guilty schoolboy skiving off. When I parked the car up I had a walk around the marina, thinking the fresh air might do me a bit of good. Eventually I found myself outside the *Minerva,* so went in.

The bar was quiet, which didn't bother me as I wasn't in a talkative mood. My head was still throbbing and my thoughts were all over the place. One pint turned into two as per usual, then I knocked back what I had left. I headed for my apartment and went straight for the medication I'd brought back with me from the hospital. Standing at the kitchen sink, I threw back a couple of industrial strength knockout pills with a glass of water. I took a couple of Tramadol through to the bedroom with me for later. Letting my clothes fall in a heap on the floor, I climbed into bed and pulled the duvet tight around me. I didn't think I'd sleep but I was going to try my damnedest.

***

The veins on the backs of my hands looked like raised contours of a map, almost ready to pop as I gripped the steering wheel. I could hardly see through the obscure patterns on the windscreen, the swirling snow in front of me was mesmerising, I was disorientated, the road in front barely visible. Pellets of ice like frozen peas battered the car; it was like being sat in a tin can and bombarded with pebbles from an automatic weapon.

I drove the car at crawling speed, hardly moving along an unclassified road, my eyes were stinging with concentration. A gateway to a field opened up on my left, I edged the car into the clearing as far as I dared. The gateway was sheltered from the maelstrom going on around me, I got out of the car into the faux lull, everywhere was glistening with ice, and more ice and covered in a thin layer of snow.

Had I been sent to this place for a reason? Maybe, maybe not, I didn't have a clue. I shut the car door and stood as the snow swirled above my head. For some reason I can't explain, I kicked my way through the snow to the five bar timber gate, I pushed, it wouldn't budge, I shoved harder, it moved. The gate juddered open, creating a glistening semi-circle of compressed snow.

By the time I'd managed to free the gate, my blue un-gloved fingers almost froze to the wooden top bar, I brought my hands to my mouth and blew into the cupped palms. My feet moved automatically, I was drawn forward, ankle deep in soft pure snow that soaked through my shoes, numbing my toes. I gasped as the freezing air caught at the back of my throat then escaped between my lips in mini clouds of freezing crystals. Through stinging, watery eyes, I could see the crescent of the moon in between the fleeting clouds. Any minute I expected to hear crazed wolves howling, I stood and listened.

Nothing. Silence.

To my left I could see the snow had blown across the open land, to form a low, undulating drift up and over what lay concealed below and between the hawthorn bushes. I kept moving forward, slowly. Perspiration froze on my brow. I fell to my knees between the hawthorns, my hands stretched out in front, my fingers dug into the frozen mound, I looked at my now blue fingers, I continued scraping as my hands revealed the secret of the drift.

***

'It's time to get up...it's half past six...it's time to get up'. Bugger! The alarm went off and I woke up sweating. What on earth was that all about? I padded through to the kitchen and noticed my car keys on the table, I never leave them there. Their home is on a hook near the front door, and that's where I found my shoes, stood in a wet puddle on the laminate flooring. Puzzled, I put the kettle on and then went back into the bedroom. I am by nature a tidy person, a home for everything and everything in its place, but on the floor was a pile of wet clothes. Now I was worried. Was it just a dream? It had to be, what else? But judging by the look of things it did seem as if I been out during the night. I've never, never, ever sleep-walked in my life, never mind driven a bloody car through a blizzard in my sleep. Puzzling.

After what had been happening inside my head over the past twenty-four hours, to say I was feeling a bit rough would be an understatement. So using, or I should say abusing, my rank, I rang the nick and asked them to send a car for me. I was surprised when Ria turned up, ringing my door bell twenty minutes later.

'Blimey, "H", you don't look so good.' Very observant, our Ria.

'Thanks for that, I don't need you to rub it in.'

'Seriously, you look like crap, Harry. Why don't you give work a miss and go back to bed?' She was genuinely concerned.

'Not to worry, I'll be ok once we get to the nick.' This I didn't believe for one minute.

'Never mind work, sit yourself down and I'll make you a cup of tea.'

I dropped down onto the sofa. 'Make it a mug will you?' I shouted through to the kitchen. Ria brought the drinks through and sat next to me.

'Don't you think you should give the doctor a ring?'

'Wedding? Engagement…?'

'For God's sake, can't you ever be serious?'

I felt a little embarrassed at the outburst.

'It's nothing—just—well I've been having theses funny turns and not sleeping too good.'

'All the more reason to see the doctor.' She picked her mug up and sipped, I did the same and tried to change the subject.

'Anyway, how come they sent you to pick me up?'

'Nobody *sent* me. I was worried after you called in yesterday to say you were going home. I thought something might be wrong.'

'Well there's no need to worry, I'll be fine when I catch up on some sleep.'

'Have it your own way.'

We sat in silence and finished our drinks. I picked up my keys as we left and shook my head, I still couldn't work out what had happened the previous night.

***

I sat in the passenger seat feeling like my head was full of cotton wool; I was thinking what a bloody good job I wasn't driving. We'd no sooner set off when my mobile rang. 'Blackburn.'

'Boss, it's Mike. Is Ria with you?'

'Sat beside me as we speak, driving like a bloody taxi driver.' She looked offended as I glanced her way. 'Reception sounds bad, where are you?'

'On the way to Killingwoldgraves Lane.'

'Where the hell is that?'

'Bottom of the Beverley by-pass, the A164. Uniform responded to a call, dog walker found the body of a young woman.'

'Ok, we'll find it, see you soon as. Ria, I hope you've got your wellies in the boot.' I told her where we were going and was quite surprised when she said she knew the place.

We turned onto the A164 towards York, and what I was feeling was really weird, like I've said before a feeling of déjà vu was hanging over me. We turned into Killingwoldgraves Lane. Jesus, it was if I was almost back inside my nightmare, but I couldn't be, could I? The hairs on the back of my neck prickled as if they were standing on end, I could feel the sweat dripping down the back of my neck.

'Are you alright, "H"?' I knew it, I bloody knew I should have listened to her and taken the day off. 'You look worse now than when I picked you up,' she said as she gave me a sideways glance.

'You worry too much, I'm tickety-boo,' I said, trying to smile. I'm a good liar. Ria drove us down the country lane. Up ahead where the road narrowed, we could see the squad cars with flashing lights. Deep snow filled the roadside ditches, heavy snow-laden branches overhung from the trees, the bare hawthorn hedges were topped with layers of glistening white and there was even the timber five-bar gate. Too real by far.

Ria pulled the car into the so-called lay-by, I stepped out into the snow, it was nearly up to my ankles so I got back in the car. Ria yelled over to a CSE to see if she could scrounge us a couple of pairs of wellies. I really needed to calm my nerves, so took my fags from my pocket and lit up. I sat blowing smoke through the open window while I waited for the nicotine to work.

Once we were suited in forensic overalls, we made our way along the cordoned off, well flattened snow path. Questy and DC Steve Wales saw us approach, so Steve stayed where he was and Questy came over.

'Alright, Mike?

'Not bad, "H", could have done without this though.'

'Couldn't we all. What have we got?' The wind started blowing up; I pulled up the hood of the paper protective suit for what it was worth, no thermal qualities whatsoever. I could feel the cold sweat freezing on my forehead and the back of my neck. Mike started blowing warm breath into his hands. I watched the CSE team down on their knees with their hands buried deep, almost up to their elbows in the white stuff, searching the area.

'Bloke over there,' he pointed towards a middle-aged man who looked as if he was wrapped up for a trip to the Arctic, holding a German Shepherd on its lead. 'The dog was free running and decided to go walkabout. Anyway, he eventually found the mutt with his head buried and scratching in a pile of snow under the bushes,' he nodded towards where the activity was taking place. 'As soon as he saw what the dog was digging at, he called it in.'

'Lead the way,' I said, very reluctantly following Questy and Ria. All I really wanted was to get back in the car and piss off home. The immediate area around the crime scene was already cordoned off, Tosh and some of his CSE team were huddled around a mound of snow below the bushes. The thing is, it was near as damn-it my dream in real life: it was happening. I'd seen enough, I knew what they'd find under the snow. Inside I was shaking like hell, but I had to carry on with the pretence. Deep breaths, I told myself, breathe deep, I hoped I looked composed and took charge of the scene.

'Questy, get back to the office to get things sorted.' There's no-one better, he's the best Murder Room Manager I've ever had. I stood by the flapping crime scene tape, reluctant to go any further, but needs must. With Ria by my side, we ducked under the tape.

Tosh Thompson, the Senior CSE, struggled in the snow as he tried to stand, like a stranded seal due to his stout physique. I was sure he knew we called him Lard Arse.

'Morning, Ria, nice boots,' he said, looking at the size nine wellies on size four feet. '"H", it's good to see you on the mend. Mind you, if you don't mind me saying you still look like a bag of shit.'

'Thank you for your concern, Tosh,' I answered sarcastically. We usually have a bit of banter, but as he said, I *did* feel like a bag of shit and couldn't be arsed.

Puffing and panting, he pulled back the hood of his protective suit to reveal his shining sweating dome and took off the paper mask. 'As you can see, we've started to clear around the body, it's slow work. We're having to almost sieve the snow from the immediate area so we don't lose any evidence. All I can tell you at the minute, is that there's a body of a young woman under there.'

Of course there was a dead girl, there had to be, but all the same, hearing him say it made my heart nearly jump out of my chest. I hadn't seen Kaja for forty-eight hours, I was praying it wasn't her. 'Nothing you can say about her yet then, Tosh?' I had my fingers and toes crossed.

'The only thing I can say for certain is that she's a blonde.'

My palpitations started to ease, Kaja is a brunette. I nodded my thanks, then started to slink away and leave him to it. I stripped off the suit and chucked it in the boot of the car, fished the fags out of my pocket and lit up. Nicotine is supposed to have a soothing effect, but I can tell you that it really is a load of bollocks. I left Ria in charge on site and signalled across to Steve Wales to give me a lift. There was still no way I was fit to drive back to the station.

When we got back to the nick, I left Steve to co-ordinate with Questy, and get the extra IT equipment sorted that was needed when we got tied up with a major investigation. Me, I needed some thinking time, and headed off to the canteen. Bren was still on shift.

'What the bloody hell have you been up to?' she asked as I made my way across to the counter, my shoes squeaking all the way. 'You look like death warmed up.' If she only knew.

'Oh come on, Bren, don't you start as well. I've just about had enough for one day.' I didn't really mean to snap at her. I didn't have to ask, she passed me a mug of tea.

'Well, what on earth are you doing at work?'

'Can't afford to be anywhere else, we've got a major enquiry starting up.' I did feel drained, Bren didn't even rollock me for leaning on the counter with my elbows, and that was a first.

'Well, if you want my opinion, you should be at home tucked up in bed.'

'Fancy tucking me in?' Usually I would mean it.

'You're in no fit state for any of that, Harry.'

I laughed and it felt good.

'Give me a yell if you want anything.' She turned and shook her head as she went back to work. It was good to have her back behind the counter.

I found myself a clear table, parked my arse next to a radiator and stared out of the dripping windows into the far corner of the car park. My thoughts were all over the place, the visions, the dreams and the new case. As the saying goes, I was well and truly fucked. I kept a low profile for the next twenty minutes before making my way to the squad room.

They say you're only as good as the team around you, well I would second that. My team was bloody good and everything was well on the way to being sorted when I walked in. The far end of our new squad room had been allotted for the investigation, a white board fixed up in place. It was still bare; unfortunately it wouldn't stay that way for long. Now the waiting began. The "Golden Hour", the first hour of any murder inquiry was paramount, but due to the snow, that went out of the window. Now we had to be patient and see what Tosh and the rest of the CSEs came up with. Questy told me the Home Office pathologist had promised to carry out the post-mortem as soon as they got back with the body, which I found very surprising, he's a right cantankerous old sod who usually pleases himself.

We busied ourselves with the mundane stuff until we had some more information; usually most murder cases are carried out in more urban perspectives, not in a bloody field covered in snow in the middle of nowhere, hence sod all to go on. The initial snowy crime scene photographs that we did have blended in with the whiteboard.

The file relating to the brothel down Coltman Street wasn't progressing much either. I'd had a team on the knock, doing house to house enquiries since first light. As it turned out, the neighbours were sick of men coming at all hours day and night and were glad to see the place shut down.

Questy had as usual taken to the role as Office Manager with ease, not that I was expecting anything less of him. Questy had enough on his plate, and until the case was brought to a conclusion, he had paired up Customs Samantha with DC Russ Stevens. Russ is a good bloke and a very experienced officer; a bit like me really, he doesn't like being fucked about. Just the man to keep Samantha in line, and the young sniffers away.

Previously Questy had tasked them to trawl through the Land Agency database, to try to find out who owned the property. We'd drawn a blank there as well: camouflaged is a good term to describe what she'd discovered, the house was registered by an off-shore company based in the Isle of Man, which in turn belonged to a holding company in the Cayman Islands, what can I say but 'same old'. We still had the Russian "house keeper" in custody and I reckoned on having another go at the turd in the morning.

I had a word with Stan, the Super, and we decided in the circumstances we should stand the team down and have an early start the next day. Nobody disagreed, what with all the white stuff about it wasn't as if we were impinging on the

"Golden Hour". Now it was a case of waiting to hear from Tosh and his CSE team, and more importantly see what came to light during the post-mortem. That was one thing I always try to shy away from, not that I was squeamish, but over the years I had seen far too many of them than could be good for one person. So I delegate, this time it was to DC Steve Wales and he wasn't over pleased when I told him to be at the morgue for 7 a.m. the next morning.

***

My evening started off pretty well, considering how I'd been feeling earlier in the day. I did the culinary thing and sorted myself some boil-in-the-bag, spag bol, washed down with a sparkling water, yes water! After last night I thought it best if I tried to ration the booze a little. Once I was fed and watered, I turned on the TV. The local news mentioned a body being found on the edges of the city. Luckily that was it, no details had been leaked, not that there were any as yet.

I left the television on for background noise and turned my big reclining chair to face out over the marina. The iced-up effect looked terrific, all sparkly and glistening, but then it's always a brilliant sight no matter what the weather and it looks even better after a drink or two. Ok so I gave in, and poured myself a large measure of Appleton's dark rum, Jamaica's finest. Glass in hand, I sat pondering over what the hell was happening to my sanity. I suppose it was down to my heart attack or the medication, something like that. But what was the snowy dream about? Dream? It was turning out to be a bleedin' living nightmare. When would it end? There was only one thing for it, I had another couple of large drams of Appleton's.

***

Apart from having a bit of a headache, I felt quite good all things considered and the next morning I was at my desk pretty early, wading my way through paperwork.

Ria came in bearing a tray of drinks. 'Where's the bacon buttie?' I asked as she plonked down the mug.

'Don't push your luck, "H". I see you're feeling better today?'

'I told you all I needed was a good night's sleep. Is Steevo back from the post mortem?' I sat back and picked up my brew.

'He's just rang in, he's on his way now.'

'What have you got Samantha and Russ on with?'

'I've managed to get some lecturer in Russian from the Uni. They've taken him for a coffee and then I thought you might like to have a go at this Alexei fella.'

'Sounds like a plan,' I said. 'And Kaja, is she still at the refuge?'

'She was last night when I checked up.'

'Ok, let me finish my brew, and then we'll see if we can get something out of that piece of Russian shit we've got in the cells.' She nodded and headed for the door. 'Let me know if Steevo gets back from the PM, will you?' I said before she closed the door.

My desk phone rang and jolted me from my thoughts. 'Blackburn.' It was the DCI—I'd been summoned. Detective Chief Inspector Stan Fellows was still housed in the main building, he wouldn't give up his smart office to join us mere mortals in the new pre-fabricated extension. I knocked on the panelled door and walked in without waiting.

The DCI was sat behind his polished hardwood desk, which was as usual clutter free, everything in its place.

'Morning, Stan,' I said as I walked in. He looked a bit on the serious side as he sat there all stern, with his chin tilted downward disappearing into his neck.

'Sit down, Harry.' A bollocking was probably on the way.

'Problem?' No coffee this time.

'I've just received the crime scene report relating to the discovery on Killingwoldgraves Lane.' Why hadn't Tosh brought it to me? It wasn't like him to skip the chain of command. 'It seems there are one or two issues that need clarifying.'

'Righto, ok.' I sat back and loosened my tie.

'Do you know this young woman?' He opened a manila folder, took out a photograph and slid it across the table towards me. She was obviously dead as a door nail.

'Can't say that I do, Stan.'

'Are you absolutely sure you haven't had any contact whatsoever with her?' I didn't like the way the conversation was going.

'Look Stan, I've already said I don't know the woman. Is this the dead girl from the field? What's all this about?' This was starting to worry me.

'According to the crime scene examiner's report, evidence was found linking you to the deceased.'

'Evidence, what type of evidence? For what it's worth, for once in my life I can't be blamed for contaminating a crime scene. I was feeling crap and kept out of the way.'

'When the body was removed, the area beneath the body was meticulously searched and evidence—'

'Sir, don't fuck me about, what did they find?' I was tensing up.

'A cigarette butt, an Embassy King size.'

'Is that all? Thousands of people smoke Embassy,' I was starting to feel relieved. 'So, that's it, a cigarette end.' I let myself relax.

Then came the bombshell.

'Not contaminated with your DNA.' I felt as if I'd been floored with a length of four-by-two timber. 'Are you still saying you don't know the girl?'

'Of course I bloody am. If I knew the girl I'd tell you.' I couldn't comprehend what was happening and sat there dumbstruck for what seemed an age. 'Find anything else?' He ignored my question.

'I'm sorry, Harry. I can't tell you anything else at this stage. I'll have to take you off the case until further investigations have been made.'

'I take it I'm under suspicion. Do I need a brief?'

'I wouldn't go that far, but I suggest you have a word with your Union Representative.'

'So I am under suspicion.' I was beyond being polite. I nearly told him to fuck off and stop pissing me about. 'You're serious aren't you? I'm under suspicion?' He didn't reply, but put the photograph back in the folder. That was my cue to leave.

I shoved my chair back so hard it nearly fell over, about turned, slammed the door shut behind me and went off in search of Sergeant Sam Kirk. It was about time the useless bugger did something useful. Kirk was the station union rep. He was behind the custody desk and I gave him the nod. He passed the lock-up keys to a young uniform and followed me out of the station. I walked towards my car, Sam climbed into the passenger seat beside me. He must have known it was serious because he didn't take the piss. I took out my Embassy, passed them across and we lit up, I took a deep drag and waited for the nicotine to hit the spot, which it never seems to do these days.

'I thought you were supposed to chuck these?' He held the cigarette up and studied it as the smoke drifted out of the opened window.

'Needs must, Sam. I've got a problem.' I took another drag.

'Ok, I'm listening.' He reclined the seat and settled back.

'Yesterday, the body of that young woman...' I trailed off and put the cigarette between my lips.

'Yeah, the young lass found in the field, what about her?'

'Stan just called me into the office and asked if I knew the girl. I told him I'd never seen her before in my life.'

'Carry on.'

'The DCI told me there was evidence found at the scene linking me to the girl.'

Sam just sat quiet. I could see the cogs going around in his head.

'And do you know the dead girl?'

'I've just said, I don't fucking know her, how many more times?'

'Calm down, don't get jumpy. What sort of evidence is he talking about?' Kirk sat forward in his seat.

'A fag end, one with my DNA on it.'

'You're having me on, surely?'

'Sam, straight up, one of my fag ends was found under the body.'

'Has he suspended you?'

'Not yet, but it won't be long. He's taken me off the case.' I threw my fag end out.

'Are you going back inside?'

'Not yet,' I said as I reached onto the dashboard for my cigarettes once again.

'Ok leave it with me for now, I'll give the Federation solicitor a ring and let you know, ok?'

'If you say so, Sam, but don't hang about.' I didn't have any words left. I eventually bit the bullet and went back inside. Sat at my desk, I gave some thought to how on earth one of my dog ends ended up not only at the crime scene but actually underneath the body. I couldn't come up with a logical explanation.

'Ria, fancy some fresh air?' I asked as she passed my open office door. She turned to look in. 'And a brew, I'm buying.'

'Steady up, "H", you feeling ok?'

'No I'm not actually. Get hold of Questy, tell him not to bring his sidekick, I'll meet you at *Babs' Baps* in five, ok?' Ria went on walkabout with her mobile stuck to her ear, trying to get hold of Questy, while I made my discreet exit through the back door of the station. *Babs' Baps* was a small café about a five-minute walk away from the station. Its real name was simply *Babs' Café*, the Baps refers to her well-endowed chest. I think she would kill us if she knew what we called the place.

The café was reasonably empty—lunch time was long gone—I ordered myself a coffee, a cappuccino for Questy and a skinny latte for Ria, then sat at a corner table with a clear view of the doorway, a typical habit for a policeman.

Questy was first to arrive. 'Cheers, Harry.' He sat opposite. I've known Mike Quest for longer than I care to remember. I'd trust him with my life. 'What's all this secret squirrel stuff about?' he said, tapping the side of his nose.

'Just hang on a bit 'til Ria gets here, I don't want to have to repeat things.'

'Fair enough.' He sat nursing his mug and staring through the window.

Ria duly arrived a couple of minutes later, sat down next to Questy and picked up her latte. 'It must be important if you've found your wallet and buying us drinks.'

'The girl found down Killingwoldgraves Lane…'

'It never clicked before but the name's pretty apt,' Questy interjected. This wasn't the time for black humour.

'As I was saying before you interrupted me, what can you tell me?' I leaned forward resting my elbows on the table. 'Has Tosh had a word with either of you about the crime scene report yet?'

'No, he usually leaves that until you've been informed,' Ria said looked questioningly towards Questy, who also shook his head.

'Have either of you been called in to see the Super?' No question about it. I'm getting paranoid. They said no in unison.

'Come on, "H", what's this all about?'

'I'm off the case.' I left it hanging there and sat back in my chair.

'You're going to have to say a bit more than that, Harry.' Questy was first to respond.

'Like I said, Stan called me in earlier; it seems some evidence was found at the scene, something that connects me with the dead girl.' It was times like this I wished you could still smoke in public places. 'According to the Crime Scene Report, one of my cigarette ends was found near the body.'

'But that was the day you were feeling crap, you never went anywhere near.' I could tell Ria was confused.

'Exactly. Then you tell *me*, why was it found *underneath* the girl?'

They both sat there dumbstruck, searching their brains for a logical explanation. There wasn't one.

'He hasn't suspended you, has he?' Questy asked, genuinely concerned.

'As we speak, no, but that could change anytime, who knows? Look all I ask is, if you happen to hear anything relevant, let me know. That is, if you're comfortable with it.'

'You don't have to ask,' Questy said and Ria nodded her agreement. I knew I could count on them both, implicitly.

I let them leave *Babs' Baps* before me, I didn't want to risk anyone seeing them leaving the café with me. There was no way I felt like going back to the office. I mentioned before I didn't like skivers and it was something I seldom did, but this was one of those times. I needed to try to get my head together. I went back to the nick but didn't go in. I went straight into the car park, got in my car and headed off home.

Chapter 10
The Gangster And The Moron

I had a phone call from Newcastle. It seemed Reeta was settling in nicely, well sort of. It turned out she was pretty popular with the punters. Since I got back I'd been keeping a low profile, not that the cops had anything on me, but best to be on the safe side. I waited until the early hours, and then visited the house where the dead girl was being stored in the chest freezer. The place was a bit posher than the one down Coltman Street, it had an integral garage with a great big fuck off chest freezer. Unfortunately for me, one of our not so bright guys, Gerry Chambers, had been on the overnight shift looking after the girls. He wasn't the sharpest crayon in the box, but he was the biggest. Punters didn't fuck with him. I backed onto the house drive with the boot of the car facing the garage door. This was going to be easy fucking peasy, or so I thought. I forgot I was working with Gerry. Chambers opened the front door and let me in, I opened the side door into the garage and flicked the light switch on and went to the freezer. I lifted the lid and a haze of condensation hit the air, I reached in and felt the body, she was as stiff as a fucking board—no, I tell a lie, she was actually curled up like a frozen snail. I told Gerry to get a blanket or something.

'Where from?'

'The *bedroom* would be as good a place as any, don't you think?' Thicko.

'What are you going to do with it?' the idiot asked when he came back. Can you believe this moron? I contemplated putting *him* in the freezer.

'She looks a bit on the cold side so I thought I'd wrap her up all nice and warm. What do think I want it for, you fucking idiot?' Wanker.

Gerry double checked that the girl didn't have any identification on her. It was a bit of a struggle with her being frozen stiff, but we eventually stripped her down to her underwear and noticed she had a small tattoo of a rose on her ankle. This was soon taken care of with a steel scouring pad. No trace left, just a bloody mess.

Anyway, me and the moron managed to get her into the boot of the car without too much trouble. I was going to do the driving. 'You just sit there and keep your gob shut,' I told him. He was obviously sulking because he actually did what he was told without arguing.

I drove the clapped-out Renault out of the city via the A164 to Beverley and turned off onto a narrow non-classified road towards Walkington. The driving conditions were pretty crap, horrendous with snow laying on top of the black ice. The arse end of the car swung about more than once or twice, and I was glad of the extra ballast in the boot. The road got narrower, the snow was building on both sides, but I kept going until I found the spot I needed. A small lay-by came up on the nearside, overhung by leafless oak trees with branches heavy with snow. I eased the car to a stop.

'Right, this'll do,' I said to dumb fuck. 'I'll open the gate and you get her out of the boot.' We were doing well, he didn't ask why. I opened the car door; my feet disappeared into six inches of snow. I shuffled through the mire and nearly did my back in as I thrashed about trying to open the five bar wooden gate; I had to get the moron to help me push it wide.

'What shall I do with her?' She was still frozen like a half side of beef.

The window was blowing from the east, drifting to the left of the gate. 'Over there,' I pointed to the hawthorn hedge. It looked hard work walking in the ankle deep snow with a corpse hanging over his shoulder, but nothing the moron couldn't handle. 'Shove her under the hedge,' I said. The way the snow was drifting it wouldn't take long to cover her. I was freezing: an Armani suit isn't made for playing snowballs in. It was funny really, I stood looking down at the naked body that lay in the snow, thinking it's a good job the girl was dead or she'd have caught her death of a cold. Ha, ha. I nearly forgot to tuck the cigarette stub under the body.

'What's all this about, boss?' The moron asked.

'Mind your own fucking business. Just do what you're told—and when we get back, keep your gob shut.' I reached into my arse pocket and took out my wallet. His eyes stared as I took out six fifty pound notes. I reached across and shoved them in his shirt pocket.

'Cheers, boss, no problem.' Money always does the trick. I let Gerry the moron drive us back in to the city, my toes were numb. The moron sat beside me complaining about his wet feet, anybody else would have just turned the car's blower on without being told.

The roads weren't quite so bad on the return trip; by the look of things the snow ploughs had been doing a cracking job of clearing things. When we got back to the house, I had a couple of whiskies to warm me up. I asked Gerry for an update on the punter who'd cost us some serious money: at least the moron got something right, he'd got the punter to sign up for a £40,000 loan with one of our subsidiary companies, using his house as collateral. It was either that, or what they used to say in the old movies he'd be getting a *pair of concrete boots.* Little did the punter know he'd be tied up to us for the rest of his life. With our interest rate, I reckon it wouldn't be too long before the house came our way.

Chapter 11
The Policeman Has Doubts

I sat in my chair, staring out of the balcony doors onto the marina, thinking. My mind was all over the place: what kept coming to the fore front was the dream, driving my car in the middle of the night, snow, ice, and a body. Had I really been out that night? Did I kill the girl? No bloody way. I searched for answers and came back at myself with more questions. Even though the problem with Kaja was sorted, the elusive smell of her perfume kept haunting me, which reminded me I hadn't been doing as much as I should have to find her sister. I made a mental note to make it a priority.

To say I was confused would be the understatement of the century. I needed to know: *had* it been a dream? Did I know the girl? And more importantly, did I kill her? Jesus Christ, what the hell was going on? How was I going to find answers to all these questions?

To hell with it, I went and poured myself a stiff drink and put the TV on to try to take my mind off things. Then I remembered about the pile of wet clothes on the bedroom floor and finding my car keys on the table, I remembered I *was* out of it, drugged up to the eyeballs, but I had no recollection whatsoever of leaving the apartment. Another drink. I sat looking out until I felt myself nodding off and headed for my bed. I could still smell Kaja's perfume as I passed the spare room.

***

I woke before any verbal assault from the alarm; surprisingly, I felt ok. I sat at the kitchen table with a mug of tea and a couple of slices of toast, listening to the early news on Radio Humberside, the local station. There were the usual stories about the depressing state of the economy; forty-six people in Hull were chasing each job vacancy. On the plus side, the new proposed Siemens Green Port on the old Alexandra Dock promised job creation: that had to be good for the city.

'Morning, Ria.' She was already hard at it in her sectioned-off part of the squad room. The lads on the night shift were few and far between, most of them had already skived off and my lot were starting to make an appearance. I tried not to show how I was really feeling, what with recent events it was bloody hard to keep it hidden when I was feeling so pissed off. 'Have you had your hair done?' I couldn't really tell but it helps now and again to keep her happy.

'No.' Sub-consciously she brought her hand up to touch her fringe. 'What are you after, "H"?'

'A bacon banjo wouldn't go amiss, with that brew we're having. Please.'

She did that shake of her head thing that she does, mumbled something and went off to the canteen.

I went into my office and got settled behind my desk ready for what the day might bring. Reluctantly I turned on the computer, put my reading glasses on, then I leafed through the overnight reports before turning my attention to the emails, which as usual were ninety percent junk.

Ria came back from the canteen, she didn't knock. I swear she really did think we still shared the office. She just pushed the door open with her arse, barged in, put the tray she was carrying down on my desk and sat opposite me. 'Where's the brown sauce? Only joking.' I added before she snapped my head off. 'Good brew this, make it yourself?' I put the mug down and bit a chunk out of the banjo.

'Never mind your stomach, have you heard anything more?'

'About what?' I picked up my sarnie and made a show of pulling a strip of fat off the bacon.

'"H"! Stop buggering about, you know perfectly well what I mean.'

I raised my eyebrows.

'I am not buggering about, because I've heard bugger all. The answer to your question is no. Now my turn, have you heard who's taking over the dead girl's case?'

'That would be me.' Questy said as he knocked and walked in. 'Sorry, "H", I couldn't help overhearing.'

'Since when did this come about?' I was taken aback.

'Since ten minutes ago. The DCI called me in as soon as I walked into the office, hadn't even taken my jacket off, explained things as best he could in an embarrassed, stuttering sort of way. I'm under his supervision of course,' he told me, touching the hair on his shirt collar. At least they hadn't brought someone in from another station.

'Has anyone seen Tosh?' I was desperate to know what was on the crime scene report.

'Seems he's keeping a low profile, Boss.'

'Aye, the bugger should do. He knows he should have tipped me the wink before running off to see Stan.'

'Keep positive, "H",' Questy said as they left the office. Fat chance of that.

They'd no sooner left my office when the internal phone started ringing. I picked it up, 'Blackburn.' Shit, it was the DCI asking me to go to his office. There was no way I could get out of it. Believe me, I tried.

Keeping up the appearance, I knocked on Stan's door and walked in as if nothing was wrong. 'Morning, Stan—' I cut it short, Detective Superintendent Raymond Mann was stood by Stan's desk and he had a face like a robber's dog.

'Sit down, Harry,' Stan said.

'It's ok, I'm fine standing.'

'The DCI told you to *sit* down.'

Bloody hell, here we go again, I sat.

The Super did not look a happy bunny. Neither was I. 'There have been further developments in the matter of the dead girl.'

'And which girl would that be?'

'Don't try to be clever, Inspector, it doesn't suit.' Ok; so no piss taking. 'Further evidence linking you to the girl has come to light.' I swear he looked as if he was enjoying taking me to task. A few years back we used to be mates, that is until he caught me copping a feel of his missus at a Christmas do.

'Can I ask what this evidence is, sir?' This was getting beyond a joke.

'I'm sorry, Inspector, at this moment in time I am not at liberty to divulge that information.' Stan didn't say a word. 'Until further investigations have been carried out, and a suitable conclusion has been reached, you are suspended from duty, effective from now. Please give me your warrant card.'

I was struck dumb; I just sat there like the village idiot. Eventually I pulled myself together, stood up, took my warrant card out of my pocket and threw it down on the desk. I didn't say a word, just turned and walked out of the office, slamming the door and making it rattle in the frame.

The supercilious twat of a Superintendent gave me fifteen minutes to clear my office of anything personal and then I was to be escorted off the premises. Bastard, wanker, toss-pot, dickhead, I called him all the names that I could think as I stomped my way back to my office slamming and banging every door I went through.

Once in the privacy of my own *'not for long'* office, I dropped down heavily in my chair wondering what the hell was happening to me. Then Stan came in, full of apologies and bullshit. He told me to take my time and try not to worry, he was sure it would all be sorted. Bollocks. Before I left the station, I managed a clandestine meeting with Questy and Ria, in of all places, the ladies' toilet. Even though they were putting their jobs on the line, they promised to keep me informed of any new developments. I did take my time, but eventually I was tracked down and duly escorted off the premises. Bastards.

***

I had a meeting with Kirk the Federation Rep, and Questy's solicitor partner, William. Initially I said I didn't need a solicitor, telling myself it would all disappear as quickly as it had happened, but Questy and Ria had been very insistent, and as far as solicitors go they don't come any better than William. I'm glad they did, because if push came to shove, it was very, very likely that I'd need a good brief.Kirk and William had put the pressure on CPS and had been granted access to all the information supposedly against me. It turned out not only was one of my fag ends found at the scene, but a couple of strands of my hair—if you can call my near skinhead cut hair—had been found on the actual body. Now all we had to do was find out how they got there, 'cause I'm sure no bugger else was going to look very hard. With a bit of skulduggery, I'd managed to photocopy the case notes on the dead girl before they tracked me down and slung me out of the nick on my ear.

Once I'd been thrown out of the office, there was precious little I could do but go home. The weather was crap, I was feeling crap, and altogether it was a crappy end to a crappy week in my crappy life. I made myself a mug of tea and settled down at the kitchen table to read the information I'd "borrowed".

According to the pathologist's report, the girl was in her mid-twenties and probably of eastern European origin. She was already dead before she was dumped in the field, obviously. The interesting thing was she'd been frozen after death and then thawed out like a ready meal. This was before she'd been re-frozen in the sub-zero temperature the evening before she'd been found. The pathologist's report also stated she had died due to "oxygen deficiency; a powerful compressive force had been applied to the thoracic cavity, in turn causing traumatic asphyxia".

I had to take a look on Google to look for a simple explanation, to put it bluntly she had been "Burked". Apparently this was the preferred method of killing of the notorious mass murderers Burke and Hare, who had supplied cadavers to the Edinburgh medical schools for research in the early 1820s. Burke and Hare would find a suitable or even a not so suitable victim, freshly dug up or alive. If the victim was indeed alive, once their victim was subdued they would simply sit on their victim's chest and literally squash the life out of them, hence the term "Burked" was born.

"Burked". How could I do that to anybody? It just didn't make any sense. I knew I could be a bit absentminded at times, but murdering a girl? That *was* surely something I'd remember, wouldn't I? Ok, so the odds were stacked against me; I couldn't argue about the DNA linking me to the girl, there was no doubt about it, but how the hell did it get there? The thing that was a big concern to me was my missing night. Car keys on the table, where they shouldn't have been, my wet clothes on the bedroom floor and no bloody recollection of the night's events.

Then the door intercom interrupted my thoughts; it was Ria, so I told her to come up.

'Holding up ok?' she asked as she came through the door.

'Aren't you supposed to be working?'

'Knocked off early, I thought you might want some company.'

'Coffee?'

'No thanks, I'll have a glass of this.' She produced a nice looking bottle of red wine from her bag.

'So that's why you women have large handbags!' I took it from her and went through to the kitchen, she followed. Ria sat at the kitchen table and spun around the file, she raised her eyebrows at me when she saw me looking.

'Took a risk, didn't you?'

'Well, I wasn't just going to sit here and let them crucify me, was I?'

'Yeah, well you don't want to get into any more bother.' Then the door intercom buzzed again. It was Kaja.

'Kaja, come in, the more the merrier,' I said as we went through to the kitchen to join Ria. 'Is everything ok?' I asked the girl, knowing full well everything was *not* ok. I got another glass out of the cupboard, poured and pushed the drink towards the girl.

'You have news about Reeta?' The question I'd been dreading. I picked up my glass and took a sip, well more of a swallow.

'The thing is, Kaja, I have a bit of a problem…I'm not actually working at the moment.' I wasn't going to go into details; she had enough on her mind. 'But I can assure you my colleagues are looking into it.' I felt guilty as hell. What with all that was happening, I'd put her sister low on my list of priorities. I tried to be tactful and changed the subject. 'How are things at the refuge, are they looking after you?' I think maybe she knew something was afoot, as she just sat there quietly. Shit, she was looking at the folder I'd carelessly left open on the table.

'I know her.' Kaja pointed and tapped the photograph in the folder. I glanced at Ria, I couldn't believe what I'd just heard.

'Sorry, what did you say?'

'Girl in picture, I know her.' She tapped again.

'How do you know her?' I could barely keep the excitement out of my voice.

'She works in house, like me.'

'Are you sure it's the same girl?' I needed to be certain.

'Of course I sure.'

'Can you tell us her name?' asked Ria.

'Olga Insk. She from Serbia. This picture, is Olga dead?'

'Yes I'm afraid she is, are you sure it's Olga?' I asked again. She didn't have to answer, her eyes filled up, it was taking her all her time not to cry. A missing sister, now a dead friend.

'Can you tell us where she lived?' Ria asked.

'She live and work in house on Boulevard.' Bloody hell, The Boulevard was only a couple of streets away from the house we shut down, what's more it was nearly on the bloody station doorstep. How the hell didn't we know about the place? 'I show you.'

Chapter 12
The Gangster Strikes A deal

The word was out on the street: a crisp fifty pound note and a nice little plastic bag of white powder and almost anything can be achieved. As usual, this proved to be the case, less than twenty-four hours after the word had been put out and one of Hull's many pissheads reckoned he had a lead on my missing girl.

I never ever, give out my mobile number to pissheads or junkies. I mean who wants scum like that giving you a bell every time they've got a few quid to spend and need a pick-me-up? Leave that to the runners, that's my motto. Somehow or another, this particular pisshead managed to get a hold of my number, I told him to lay off the shit and to meet me in the *Rose* pub later that afternoon.

I didn't actually know the bloke I was meeting, I reckoned he'd be easy to pick out because the *Rose* isn't the typical junkie type of pub. As soon as I opened the pub door I saw him, he stood out like a vicar in a brothel nursing a half of something. The regulars were giving him a wide berth. I realised why as I got closer: he stank like a sewer, I'm surprised he hadn't been thrown out on his arse.

I ordered a dram of whiskey for myself and a pint for the pisshead, I didn't intend hanging about any longer than I had to, he looked contagious: like he had scabies or something more deadly.

He told me he'd been doing a bit of begging at the top end of Whitefriargate in the old town when he saw her. He followed her down the side of the marina and watched her going into an apartment block about halfway down Prince's Dock Side. It had to be the copper's place. Anyway, he'd pooled all his remaining brain cells and came up with a plan.

He waited for her to leave and subsequently followed her to a women's refuge at the town end of Springbank Avenue.

He sat there, smiling through his stained, broken teeth, as I passed him his reward under the table along with a fifty pound note. He thought all his birthdays had come at once. One thing I did do, before I left him to piss the money up the wall, and that was to take his mobile from him and delete my number. I didn't want any social calls.

Now it was my turn to formulate a plan. I wanted the whore back, pronto. Just to be on the safe side I decided to get the place checked out. The pisshead would be sorry if he'd sold me a dud. I got one of my lads to keep an eye on the place. The big problem was that with it being a refuge for slags, security was usually pretty good, they were always on the lookout for dodgy blokes loitering. I needed to know for definite she was there and I needed to know her routine. We were going to pick her up but that was for another day in the near future, tonight I had a date.

It was good every now and then to get away from all the everyday shit. Don't get me wrong, I enjoy my work—if you can call it work—but just once in a while it's nice to be normal. I'd met this girl quite by accident, doing a bit of shopping along Newland Avenue and being hassled by one of these aggressive beggar types. Being the gentleman that I am, I stepped in and told him none too politely to fuck off. She told me to mind my own business and that she could handle it, then she tripped over a paving slab as she turned to walk away. I helped her to her feet and this time she was a bit more polite, a bit of small talk followed by a coffee and you know the rest.

Chapter 13
The Policeman's Sanity Returns

As Ria would be driving, she swapped her wine for coffee while Kaja told us a bit more about her life before she came to England. It was a familiar story, a poor family, very little in the way of decent job prospects, hence the need to respond to a dodgy internet ad offering jobs with prospects and we know what happened next. We finished our drinks, and with Ria behind the wheel, we headed out for a drive down the Boulevard. Kaja pointed out the house. It wasn't dissimilar to the one down Coltman Street, a large three storied terraced place in need of a little TLC. There was bugger all I could do but hand the whole thing over to Questy and Ria. I was suspended, after all.

'Olga.' I said out loud. 'Why on earth would someone try to frame me for your murder? And how did they get hold of the so-called "evidence"?' I started to think maybe I *was* tied up in this somewhere, again the question, but why? First off there was Kaja, her missing sister, us closing down their place of work and now me, framed for the murder of their "colleague", Olga. This may be the line I should be thinking along, getting my comeuppance.

***

There was no question about it: I owed Kaja a massive debt. The problem was now that I'd been suspended, how was I going to repay it? I decided a bit of fresh air might be what I needed. Seeing as though I hadn't been keeping up with my exercise regime, I togged up and off I went. It was still crap weather, the sleet was like icy needles attacking my face, blowing almost vertically off the river. I set off into a head wind with my head down and arms pumping, I tried doing my power walking, bugger the jogging. Regardless of the weather, I always consider myself lucky living where I do, close to the city centre, with the marina and river front almost on my doorstep.

By the time I plodded my way down the quayside to the old Victoria pier, I was fair gasping for breath; I could tell I'd let the exercise lapse, I was knackered. The wind and sleet hadn't eased at all as I stood bent over, trying to get my breath back, resting my hands on my knees. As far as I could see I had two choices, a pint in the *Minerva* or a cup of tea in the pier café; for once I did the sensible thing and chose the latter.

I was sat nursing a cup of weak tea, looking out of the picture window across to Barton on the other side of the Humber, when my thoughts were interrupted.

'Harry! I haven't seen much of you since you got back to work.' It was Captain Derek, owner of the *Dancing Lady* which was berthed right opposite my apartment.

'Hello, Derek, I never saw you come in, I was miles away.'

'Mind if I join you?' Captain Derek was already pulling out a chair. 'How are you, Harry, are you back at work full-time?' He's such a nosey bugger.

'I'm not doing so bad, thanks, and yes I'm back at it catching the bad guys.'

'Did you catch that chap the other night?'

'And what chap would that be, Derek?'

For some reason, he laughed. 'You know, last Tuesday night, that little so and so who was trying to steal your car, of course.'

He must have thought I was barmy from the expression on my face. I didn't have a clue what on earth he was on about.

'Oh, him,' I racked my brain until it hurt, well I would have if you could do such a thing, my memory was shot.

'If you hadn't come out to investigate when you did— well, who knows what might have happened.'

'Still working on it, I can't understand what anyone would want with my old Ford,' I said to him, then I had a flashback. It was the day that I'd had that "episode", the result of which I'd gone to bed half pissed and full of Tramadol.

We sat and talked about the weather, obviously, and the *Dancing Lady*. As soon as I thought enough time had lapsed to excuse myself, I said my cheerios. Desperation was taking over, I needed to call Questy and Ria. At least now I had an inkling what had happened. The good thing is, this went a long way towards explain my wet clothes on the floor and the misplaced car keys. Maybe I didn't have anything to do with Olga's death. Joy! One question remained to be answered, why would anyone one want to nick my car? As I walked back to the apartment, I gave Questy a call on the mobile and told him the news.

That evening, when they'd finished work for the day, Questy and Ria picked up a take-away for us all and came around to the apartment. We sat at the kitchen table which was littered in foil dishes full of oriental delicacies. I have to admit, it was a change, made more enjoyable by the fact I didn't have to get my wallet out. They made up for it by supping their way through my wine and beer as we tried to make some sense of what Captain Derek had told me.

'Ok then, "H", supposing, just supposing, this bloke did manage to get inside your car, why didn't he nick it?' Questy asked.

'I'm telling you Mike, it wasn't the car he was interested in. He had no intention of nicking it.' We'd been at it a while and I needed a smoke; I took one out of the packet and opened the French door to the balcony.

'Harry, do you have to?' Ria said as she grabbed at the file on the table. It was making an excellent effort of trying to escape through the opened window.

'Look,' I said, ignoring her. 'It all makes sense, or no sense whatever. Some little shit breaks into my car, grabs a fag end out of the ashtray and plucks a couple of hairs off the headrest. The thing I don't know is, why try and set me up?' I stubbed out the fag, went back inside and closed the doors. The curtains were still just about in place. 'And don't forget, we have a witness, Captain Birdseye, he saw the whole episode.'

'I don't want to put a damper on things, "H", but unless we can prove someone did actually gain access to your car, we still don't have a leg to stand on.'

'Mike, why have you got to be so pessimistic?' At least Ria was on my side.

'Just get Tosh and his crime scene boffins to have a look at it, will you?' I asked him, I'd have begged if I had to. Ria gave Questy one of those looks, the disapproving type she'd been giving me for years.

'OK, let's do it.'

Yes I thought, a result! At least we might get somewhere now. The rest of the evening was taken up with small talk and more alcohol. It must have been getting on for midnight when Ria called for a taxi and they left me alone, trying to get my head around it.

The next morning there hadn't been any noticeable improvement in the weather, it was awful. By the time Tosh and his team turned up with a low-loader to take my car away for scrutiny, the sleet was blowing almost vertical off the marina. The CSEs had the luxury of wet weather gear, there was no way I was going out in that lot. I stood and watched the goings-on from the apartment lobby.

'If you'd given me call I'd have brought it down to the nick and saved you a trip,' I said to Tosh.

'Bloody hell, Harry, you of all people should know better. You're the one who's insisting that we have a look at the flaming thing and here you are wanting to cover it with even more finger prints and God knows what.' I thought he was going to blow a gasket.

'Calm down, Tosh, don't burst a blood vessel on my account. Come on up and we'll have a coffee.'

'Cheers, that's very civil of you considering.'

'Considering what?' I knew what he meant but I wasn't going to make it easy for him.

'You know, going behind your back, not telling about the evidence and the like.'

'Oh the *evidence*, you mean the fag end and the hairs you found, that just happened to belong to me and you went right above my head without saying fuck all to me, Questy or Ria?'

'Harry, what can I say? You've got me bang to rights—'

'Yes I have. Now let's go inside and have that coffee.' I forgave him, sort of. He'd done it by the book. As it turned out, the offer of coffee was a big mistake; I hadn't noticed that his crew had finished loading the car and were following us inside. 'Take your bloody boots off *and* the jackets,' I yelled as they piled into my home, dripping wet through. Next thing they'd taken over the kitchen, mugs out, biscuits eaten and the buggers even found my Battenberg cake. Still, Tosh, who had already parked his lard arse, promised that they would give the car priority and he'd get one of his team on it ASAP. I couldn't ask for more. He owed me one and he knew it. The crime scene gang eventually departed for the nick, but not before they'd just about eaten me out of house and home. Gannets.

Once they'd left and I was stuck in limbo, I got to thinking what if they didn't find anything with the car and it was all in my imagination, then I'd be right up shit creek. It was a long twenty-four hours before my phone rang.

'Blackburn residence,' I answered, half expecting it to be Questy or Ria, as not many people ring me.

'Harry.' Talk about making a tit of yourself, it was the DCI.

'Oh, sorry about that, Stan, what can I do for you?' I tried to sound respectful.

'Have you got anything on this afternoon?'

I wanted to say, "only cutting my toe nails". 'Why, am I going to be sacked or something?'

'There's no need to try to be funny. My office, two o'clock this afternoon. There's been developments.'

'What developments?' I wondered what the hell I'd done now.

'It'll save. Two o'clock, don't be late.'

I wasn't going to rush my bollocks off getting there for two o'clock, why the hell should I? I know it was childish but that's me all over. I thought "in for a penny, in for a pound", so I put my waterproofs on and went for a couple of pints in the *Minerva*. It was pretty quiet in the pub, no big rush on, so I thought I'd treat myself to a jumbo sausage, chips and curry sauce, just to keep me going.

The time eventually came when I had to leave the sanctuary of the pub and go and listen to Stan's words of wisdom, ha! We had been mates for years, but now? I wasn't so sure any more. Seeing as though I had no car until the CSEs had finished their examination, I had to call a taxi, which arrived twenty minutes later than it should have. The result of my lunch and the late arrival was that I was well and truly unfashionably late for my meeting with the DCI.

'You wanted to see me, sir?' I kept it formal, no taking the piss, which was hard as he didn't look as if he wanted to be there.

'Harry, glad you made it … eventually.' Sarcastic bugger. 'First off, a statement was taken from that neighbour of yours, the one who lives on a yacht—'

'It's a launch, sir.' I kept emphasising the sir, just to make a point.

'Whatever, what he told us does seem to confirm your theory.' His bullet head was starting to glisten with sweat.

'And what theory would that be, sir?' I wasn't going to make it easy for him.

'About your car being broken into to remove articles that could be used against you.'

'Articles; you mean the fag end and a couple of hairs?' I enjoyed seeing him squirming in his seat.

'Yes, that's exactly what I mean. The forensic people have made a thorough examination of your car, and it appears as you quite correctly surmised that the vehicle was interfered with.' Why didn't he just say some little shit had broken into it? 'Two clear prints were found, thumb and forefinger, on the inside of the door pillar.'

'Did they manage to get an ID on who they belong to?'

'They belong to a Darren Taylor, but here's where we have a problem, Taylor has been flagged up by Serious Crimes, so it's hands off I'm afraid.'

'Do we know anything at all about Taylor?'

He peered over the top of his glasses. 'DS Middleton is doing some digging.'

'Where does this leave me, still in the shit? Sta—Sir?' I just managed to stop myself; I wanted to keep up the pretence of being pissed off with him.

'Your suspension has been rescinded forthwith, needless to say without a blot on your record.'

He was being such a pompous twat as he sat there beaming from ear to ear waiting for my response. What did he want me to say? "Oh thank you so much for clearing my name, I'll be forever in you debt?" Well he could go and shag himself, he wasn't getting one. I sat and waited for him to carry on. The silence was a long one, but eventually I won.

'As of now you are back on full duties.' He passed me my warrant card. I stood up and gave him a nod. I was just about to leave his office when he piped, 'Inspector, I expect to be kept up to speed with any developments.' Wanker. I didn't answer and kept on walking.

'Wakey, wakey,' I said loudly as I walked into the squad room for the first time in a week.

Ria stuck her head around the cubicle she shared with Questy. 'Harry, you're back!' I could have given her a sarcastic answer but I'd had enough of that for one day.

'So it would seem. Canteen?'

'If you're paying.'

'Questy about?' I asked as we walked across the car park to the main building.

'He's taken a day's compassionate leave, something to do with the divorce.'

I went to the counter and got us a couple of drinks, Bren wasn't working, more's the pity: I always looked forward to the banter. I sat there nursing my brew while Ria brought me up to date with the goings on. 'What do you know about this Darren Taylor?'

She took out her note book. 'Thirty-nine years old, likes to think he's a bit of a gangster, when he's only a low life piece of piss.' I raised my eyebrows. 'Burglar and drug dealer, he did a two year stretch in HMP Leeds for GBH.'

'Bring him in.'

'Now that is a bit tricky, "H". He's been flagged up by Serious Crime.'

'So I've been told.'

'You already knew? Thanks for sharing the information.'

'Sorry. You know, with what's been going on, it slipped my mind.'

She was seriously pissed off, almost sulking.

'Suppose you already know about John Shaw as well?'

'And who is John Shaw?'

'That's it, "H", he's well under our radar, the name came up alongside Taylor's. I can't find out anything about him, he must be into some seriously heavy stuff.'

'Until we're told anything different, I don't give a toss about who's flagged him up or who hasn't, bring this Taylor in, and get Steevo to see if he can dig anything out about this Shaw bloke.'

I needed a breather, so I put on my big coat, grabbed my fags and headed for the smokers' shed in the car park. It was bloody freezing, I sat on the bench with my head resting back on the plastic, cupping my cigarette between my hands. It was good to be back.

Chapter 14
The Gangster Reveals All

What a bloody shambles. With all that was happening of late, I'd reluctantly had to let my boss know, and we came up with a cunning plan. What is it that they say: "the best laid plans" and all that? Whatever it means, all I knew was that our cunning plan wasn't so cunning after all, it backfired big time.

The plan had been relatively simple: break into Blackburn's car, pick up a couple of bits of stuff and leg it. Well, so far so good. Before me and the moron dumped the girl, I'd put a couple of hairs taken from the headrest in Blackburn's car in her knickers, I told my man to make sure he found a cigarette butt, so when we'd got rid of her body in the snow I placed the dog end under the girl. Bye, bye Blackburn, payback time.

My *confidential* contact at the nick confirmed they'd been found and the so-called evidence pointed all the way to Blackburn. I was pleased to hear the result was that Blackburn was suspended. Yes. You may be wondering why was I setting Blackburn up? Well, not only had he found my girl a place of so-called safety, he was ruining the bloody business, on top of which he was the reason my employer had to do a runner and leave the country. It was payback time. Little did I know that the escapade of Darren Taylor getting into his car had been witnessed, bummer. Apparently, my associate Taylor had left a couple of beautiful fingerprints for the police. If only the sod hadn't been so careless, I could have seen Blackburn doing some serious time.

I'd already set the wheels in motion to keep an eye on Kaja, I wanted her back one way or the other. I'd had a team of my lads on roster system watching the refuge day and night to see if she had established a routine, unfortunately she hadn't. I could soon make up any financial losses that we'd incurred, but the girl definitely needed teaching a lesson. There was nothing else for it: I'd get her back—or maybe … I thought, yes, that was the way to go after all. If she was removed permanently, it would serve as a lesson to the other girls.

Two hours later, I was ready to sort the little whore once and for all. The refuge she was living in was about half way down Peel Street, off Springbank Avenue, a busy road into the city centre. I had a word with the moron and he supplied me with an old Renault Laguna bought off eBay. All the original identification marks had already been removed, and to be on the safe side I had him swap the number plates.

I was ready to go. I drove down to the bottom of Peel Street, turned the vehicle around, then sat and weighed up my options. The house was about two thirds up, so I drove a little further and waited.

Time went by slowly and I was starting to think maybe tonight wasn't to be, then I saw her come out of the refuge. She checked the door was locked behind her and looked up into the security camera and gave it a cheeky wave. So confident; who the hell did she think she was? She definitely needed to be taught a lesson. No other jumped-up little bitch would get above their station once they found out, which they would.

Ok, so what I was about to do came within my job description, I didn't have to enjoy it… but I did like it.

This was not the type of thing I had to do on a regular basis, which was why I was starting to sweat a little. The adrenaline was starting to surge through me, nevertheless I was well focused on the job ahead. I watched her take the three steps down to the pavement. The street was empty barring Kaja. Click, ignition on, I eased the Laguna away from the kerb, nice and steady, easy on the gas. The car crawled up the street. When I was about ten metres in front of her, I pulled up and checked the mirrors: still no-one about. I kept the engine running, got out of the car and stood by the open door, my right arm down by my side. A quick look left and right, still nobody about. Kaja was no less than six steps away, as she reached me I turned towards her, looked her straight in the face and smiled. You should have seen the look on her face, it was like that television show *Surprise, Surprise.* It soon turned to one of horror: she glanced down and watched as I slipped the six inch blade down the sleeve of my jacket, and with hardly any effort it made short work of her clothing on its way into her stomach. This was something I was pretty well practised at. I grabbed her close to me as I gave the blade an upward thrust and twist, nice. As the tension drained away I wanted to laugh out loud, I withdrew the blade as she clutched her stomach and slipped to the pavement.

'Bye, bye, whore.' She didn't answer. Ha, ha, ha.

I slung the knife into the foot-well of the car. Keeping cool, easy does it, I got back in the Laguna and closed the door quietly and drove away, I didn't even look back in the rear view mirror. There was only one job left, to get rid of the car and that was a job for the moron. I had a date to keep.

Chapter 15
A Worrying Time For The Policeman

Due to the fact I'd been late for my meeting with the DCI, followed by a quick catch up with Ria, there wasn't much of the working day left, so I headed off home. I just couldn't be bothered with cooking. I was getting worse, my diet was nearly back to what it used to be: fish and chips from the chippie.

I sat at the kitchen table and gorged myself on haddock and chips, smothered in salt and vinegar with a large dollop of tomato ketchup, made complete with a couple of slices of white bread and butter and a mug of strong tea: my idea of gourmet heaven. It was about 7.30 p.m. when the call came: Kaja had been stabbed, but she was still alive. With no respect for the city speed limits, I clogged it to the infirmary. My hospital phobia left me as I dumped the car in the ambulance bay and ran into the Accident and Emergency Department. It was heaving with casualties of one kind or another, people nursing broken limbs, the usual cuts and bruises, with hospital security keeping an eye on the drunks.

I flashed my warrant card at everyone who got in my way. I asked at the reception desk about Kaja but no-one seemed to know what was happening. A young doctor went past, so I grabbed him by the arm, only to be with threatened with security. Once I explained the position and who I was, he went to find out what he could. It wasn't welcome news, she was in a critical condition and already in the operating theatre. The young doc told me it would be some time before they knew anything more and things didn't look too good. I owed her so much.

I had a word with the uniforms first on the scene, apparently nobody had seen a thing. Kaja had been found by one of the other girls from the refuge, who was returning from visiting her mum.

I parked my arse on a plastic chair in the waiting area, with a cup of stewed hospital coffee, getting cramp in my cheeks and called the nick from my mobile for an update. The street had been sealed off, Tosh and his team were on the way to the incident and the door to door knock had already started. I sort of owed it to the girl to hang around, even though I was itching to get stuck into the case; not that I didn't have enough on my plate already.

Two hours I sat there, getting pins and needles in my arse, before the doctor came back with the news. Kaja had made it through the operation, but she was still critically ill, and it all depended on how she did over the next twenty-four hours. They wouldn't let me see her, as she was being kept in a medically-induced coma to help reduce shock, so I said my thanks to the medics and left.

I didn't go into the nick. Instead, I went straight to the scene, to be greeted by the familiar sight of flapping blue and white crime scene tape and blue flashing lights. Of course there was the usual gaggle of busybodies trying to see what was going on, a couple of uniforms were doing a good job of keeping them well back. I flashed my warrant card to the uniforms, signed the crime scene attendance log and ducked under the tape. I wasn't expecting to see Ria tonight but she was already there, someone had tipped her the wink. She didn't know the full story of what had been going on with me and Kaja, but I think she had an inkling something was afoot.

I could see Tosh had set up an interior cordon directly where the incident had taken place.

'I don't remember you being rostered on nights?' I said to Ria.

'I'm not. The night shift gave me a call, thinking I'd want to know, so here I am.'

'Thanks for that. Right, where are we at?'

'Tosh has had the full area videoed, still pictures etc, and as you can see they've started with the fingertip search.'

'Anything come up from the door to door?'

118

'Not yet; still early days, still hopeful.'

'What about CCTV?' I asked as I glanced up and down the street.

'The refuge camera is directly above the entrance door, it's mainly for checking out who's trying to get access to the building. The peripheral vision of the camera is next to useless.'

I'd noted a few of the premises down the street had their own CCTV systems, and told her to get uniform to have a word with the householders so we could have a look-see. 'Come on then, let's go and have a word with the women inside the refuge to see if anyone can throw some light on things.'

Talk about hostile, some of these women were real men haters. Bloody hell, we were only trying to help one of their own. Talk about George Orwell, every inch of the interior was covered by security cameras. Outside, around the back, the enclosed garden was also well covered, pity about the front of the building.

The refuge was the temporary home to fifteen women of different ages and four children, no-one had a clue what had happened. The lady supervising the house said the last she saw of Kaja was when she looked up into the CCTV camera and gave her a wave. All told, nothing new was gleaned. Everyone had been busy or watching television. I'd have thought there would have been one nosey bugger looking to see what was happening on the street. Now it was a case of waiting to see if the CSEs found anything and hopefully the other street residents' CCTV might have caught something. But I wasn't too optimistic.

I pulled out my mobile and gave the hospital a call to see if there was any news on Kaja. Still no change. There was little I could do at the scene, Ria had everything under control and a glass of something alcoholic beckoned, so I headed off home, leaving my DS and the uniforms to get on with things.

I got back to the apartment and poured myself a dram. What a right mess this was turning into. Girl missing, another girl dead, me being set up—and now attempted murder on Kaja. I doubted if I'd get off to sleep.

I was about three parts pissed when I decided enough was enough and went to my bed. I lay there with my duvet pulled across me, pondering the events and eventually my eyes started to close. I drifted off, wondering what the morning would bring.

The morning came, bringing with it no improvement in the weather, it was a bastard of a day. I went to the bathroom and was in half a mind to get back in bed but needs must, too much happening.

On the way to the nick, I did a drive past the crime site down Peel Street. The rather pissed off looking uniform on the door looked absolutely frozen. He said it had been an uneventful night. I told him to call it a day and gave him a lift back to the nick. I'd get Sergeant Kirk to get one of his lads to do an hourly drive past just in case, the story of my life: *just in case*.

Having a team canvassing the street residents' CCTV turned out to be next to useless, many were just dummy cameras, others didn't work or have any recording facilities. There was just one that might have something useful worth looking at. Technical had set us up with some equipment in one of the interview rooms. On the computer monitor, grainy black and white footage jumped all over the place. Still it was better than nothing and it did have some interesting images. The view was from some distance away and it showed what looked like an old model Renault. It picked the car up as it passed then went out of view, but about ten minutes later the car drove back up Peel Street and parked up with the driver's side to the kerb, right where we assumed the attack happened. The driver's side door opened and a there was a grainy image of someone climbing out, leaving the door open. Seconds later, the figure got back in and drove away. 'Steve, zoom in see if you can make out the number plate,' I asked DC Wales.

'Still no good, Boss, can't read it.'

'Hang on Steve, just go back a bit.' He hit the rewind button. 'Stop—there, you see?'

'See what?'

'That's a man's back, you can just make out the shoulder profile.'

'If you say so, Boss.' He wasn't convinced.

'Yes I do say so, get the thing to technical and see if they can clean it up a bit.' Ye of little faith duly took the tape through to IT.

Questy was back from his compassionate leave. Can sorting out a divorce come under that heading? Anyway, he'd taken Samantha to the council-run CCTV control centre, and it seemed they might have come up with something. I commandeered the same interview room we'd used before to watch the DVD they brought back with them. Samantha brought the coffee and Mike brought the popcorn, well choccy biscuits. Interestingly, an old Renault Laguna was seen driving out of Peel Street about the time of Kaja's attack. The car turned left towards the city centre and we were able to keep tabs on it right through the one way system, then we lost it for a few minutes around Queens Gardens, then we had it again. And this time the number plate was visible. The plate was registered to a Mr Frank James. The trouble was it belonged on a Ford Fiesta, bummer.

There is no getting away from CCTV cameras in this city, we were able to follow the vehicle through the city centre and double back on itself and witnessed its fiery destruction underneath the Anlaby Road flyover, very near to the KC Stadium. Eureka, we had a reasonably clear image of the bloke setting the fire. He hadn't counted on the camera pointing outward from the KC car park entrance. He was a big lad, around six feet tall, and looked like most of the others we'd come across in the investigation, the usual bodybuilder type, so full of steroids that his thighs rubbed together when he walked and his muscular arms looked as if he was ready to draw a pair of six guns. The good thing was, we were able to get a good look at his face: the usual shaved head—a large head I might add—which due to his physique looked small in comparison to the rest of him, earring in his left ear. We had a full on mug shot, now we just had to find out who the bugger was. He was bound to have a criminal record.

Ria came through to the office bearing gifts, a hot drink and a chocolate éclair. 'You do know I'm not supposed to indulge myself don't you?' I picked up the éclair.

'I won't tell if you don't.' Ria said, pulled out a chair and sat down.

I'd already had a big bite and I could feel the cream on my chin.

'Can't seem to dig much up on Taylor. He may be small time but he's got some big connections.'

'Let's bring Taylor in.'

'What about Serious Crimes, shouldn't we let them know?' she asked me.

'The DCI has probably told them already, brownie points and all that. To be honest with you, Ria, I don't give a toss about Serious Crimes or the DCI, I want Taylor picked up, end of. I did mention this before, I believe?' She didn't reply.

'Well, here's something you don't know, there is a tenuous link to Osbourne.'

Well, well, well, now this was a turn up for the books that I wasn't expecting. Osbourne was the central player in our last major investigation, a very intense case. I blamed the bastard for the stress that caused my heart attack. The bugger wouldn't get away this time. I'd make sure of it one way or another.

***

The day had ended on a strange note to say the least, and the night had the beginnings of being even stranger. I sat in my chair staring out at the winter night with all sorts of peculiar thoughts going through my head, visions of my mother's funeral, me gasping for breath, the dead girl in the snow and then another funeral, but whose? I didn't know; all these disturbing questions challenged my sanity. Were they indistinct, eerie, recollections of my past? Or maybe the future? I didn't know, I still don't.

Unusually for me, I fell asleep in my chair and stayed there all night. I woke with a blinding headache and ached all over like buggery. On the plus side, the weather had taken a turn for the better. Clear bright blue sky. Life, such as it was, was looking good. I rang the hospital before I left for work. There had been a significant improvement in Kaja's condition and if she carried on improving, they would reduce the medication that was keeping her comatose. So it was off to the nick.

I'd no sooner got myself sorted when Steve Wales knocked once on the door and stuck his head around the frame. 'Morning, Boss, we've been around to Taylor's place, there's no sign of him, I reckon he's done a bunk.'

'Any good news?' I asked.

'As it happens there is. We have an ID for the attacker of the stabbed girl.' He was well pleased, so was I. I didn't think we'd get a result as quick as this.

'Good man, who is it?'

'The mug shot we had from when he set the fire, I entered his details in the PNC and we got a hit. He doesn't have a record, but he is known in connection with plenty of buggers who do have.'

'Name? Address?'

'Gerry Chambers, twenty-eight years old, he's a licensed doorman and does casual work as a bouncer around the city. He has a flat over a block of shops on Gypsyville, 16A.'

'Right then, sort out a car, I'll let Ria know and meet you in the car park. I'm looking forward to this.' I had time for a quick smoke in the plastic shed, followed by an extra strong mint before I tracked her down in the custody suite.

'Ready for a trip out?' I asked.

'Where are taking me, anywhere nice?'

'Bloody hell, Sergeant, it's not a date,' I joked.

'Just my luck.'

If only I'd been twenty years younger and my circumstances had been different. 'Just get your coat.'

'Yes, sir,' she said as she walked away. She has a way of saying sir that gets right up my nose and she knows it.

Steevo was ready and waiting with the engine running, we timed it just right as the car had warmed through nicely. It didn't take long to get to where Chambers lived, less than ten minutes from the office. Steve parked the car around the back of the shops, and after a quick recce of the place, we found there was only one way in or out, a metal fire-escape-cum-staircase around the back.

You only have to take one look at Steve to know he spends a lot of his spare time in the gym, so obviously I let him take the lead. He bounded up the staircase like I used to do at his age and hammered on the door with his fist.

'Steve,' I said. 'Just ring the bell like any civilised person would.'

He gave me a contemptuous look and hammered again. We stood there about five minutes with Steve trying to break the door down with his bare hands.

'Hang on, no need to break the bloody door down,' a voice shouted out to us. 'Sorry about that, I was in the loo,' Chambers said as he opened the door. 'Oh shit,' he added when he saw who it was.

I pushed my warrant card into his face and I bet he'd wished he'd stayed in the toilet. I couldn't be arsed with hanging around while a warrant to search was authorised, but I can be very persuasive when I want and he stood aside to let us in. He might have been a big bloke but I think he was really a bit of wimp.

'DI Blackburn,' I said. 'Do you mind if we come in?' Chambers gave no objections and stepped aside. In comparison with his size, the flat looked tiny, a magnolia painted box. I think that's why he went for the minimalistic look with the furnishings. There was bugger all furniture in the living room except a big—and I mean big—easy chair facing a flat screen television fixed on the wall above the fireplace.

What did look out of place was the Christmas tree still standing in the corner; it was February for goodness sake! I was surprised how obliging Chambers turned out to be, no arguing, or demanding his brief like they do on the telly, nothing. I'm sure that was due to us following the smell of petrol into his bedroom and finding a pair of petrol soaked trainers. Ria read him his rights and we all went back to the car park, Chambers shrugged Steve's hand away when he held his head to stop it banging on the doorframe. I bet you've guessed, he gave it one almighty crack as he got it the car, it was that loud it made me cringe.

***

Later, in the interview room, Chambers sat across the table from me and Ria, I made my usual pretence of reading the folder that lay on the table before me, while Ria reminded him he was still under caution.

'You haven't got a couple of aspirins have you?' he asked. I couldn't stop the smile that crept across my face.

'All in good time, you'll live,' I said. I took the still photographs copied from the CCTV camera, laid them out on the Formica top and pushed them towards Chambers. 'Now what can you tell me about these?' I tapped them. 'Is this you in the photographs?

Eyes down, he looked for a few seconds and looked up. 'I could say it's our kid, but then again he only weighs eight stone wet through and he's in Wakefield nick. Of course it's fucking me.'

'In that case can you tell me what you were doing down Peel Street at approximately 7.30p.m. last night?'

'No.'

'And why not?' Ria asked him.

'Because I've never been down Peel Street.'

I showed him the video still of the car turning onto Springbank. 'That's your car?'

'No.'

Here we go again.

'It's not your car?' My patience was wearing a bit thin.

'It belongs to a mate.' The cocky sod smiled as if the comment was going to let him off the hook.

'If it belongs to a *mate*, why did you torch it? Not a very nice thing to do.'

''Cos he asked me to.'

'Do you always do what your mates ask?'

'This one you do, don't ask questions just do it.'

'And does this mate have a name?' I wasn't banking on getting an answer.

'What, do you think I am stupid or summat? I like living too much.'

'So, if you're not going to tell us who the car belongs to, that puts you in the frame, and I don't mean setting the fire.'

'Frame for what?' He looked a bit worried this time.

I took off my specs and placed them down with exaggerated care, letting his question hang there. I sat back in my chair, folded my arms across my chest.

'Well?' he asked.

I kept quiet and looked to Ria.

'Attempted murder,' she told him.

'Now hang on, attempted murder? Me? You're having a laugh.' He was starting to sweat. Globules formed on his bald head and began a trickling journey down his face, and he wiped them away with the back of his hand.

I sat forward in the chair, resting my elbows on the table. 'Do I look as if I'm laughing? The car was seen driving away from an unsuccessful murder attempt on a young woman. As you've already admitted, it was you in the photograph torching the car; on top of that we have your petrol soaked trainers. It doesn't look too good for you, from where I'm sitting.'

'You do realise if I tell you who asked me to do it that I'm a dead man?' Now the pressure was on, he was starting to sweat heavily and he didn't half pen and ink.

'We can give you protection,' Ria told him.

'Yeah right, as if.'

'Look, as I see it, if you don't tell us the name of your mate, you'll be going down for a very long time.' He went quiet and seemed to be pondering on what I'd said.

'If I give you his name, I want a brief here, 'cos I want the protection stuff in writing.' Brief, I ask you, they all say brief, too much telly. Chambers was duly taken to one of our best suites to await the duty solicitor.

'I'm going for a fag,' I said to Ria.

'They'll be the death of you, those things,' she scolded. If only she knew.

I was feeling a bit woolly headed, so I went back to the office and grabbed my top coat. I hoped a walk around the block might clear my head. I had every intention of just going to the shed for the unclean, but somehow found myself in *Babs' Café*. With weak cup of coffee in front of me, I sat looking out of the window, staring at the sleet as it hit the window in star formations and dispersed into rivulets, which ran down the plate glass. Detached from my surroundings, it was if I was watching through a third person. Through the grey, sleet sky I could see blue, soft, white fluffy clouds and green grass, arms stretched out I could see myself as I lay on the grass watching the cloud formations … I was miles away.

'Harry, Harry?' The voice was familiar but distant. It was the hand shaking my shoulder that brought me out of my reverie. 'So here you are, I've been looking all over for you, you've been gone ages.' Ages? I looked at my watch. I'd been away for more than a bloody hour, how did that come about?

In the hour that I'd gone walkabout, the duty solicitor had turned up and was going ballistic about having to hang about waiting. When we got back to the nick he was fuming.

'Inspector, don't you think I have better things to do with my time than—' I cut him short and apologised, making the excuse that something vitally important which needed my immediate attention had come up. Ria stood there gobsmacked as I went into my spiel.

I don't know why he'd kicked off. After all, he was getting paid for hanging around and the actual interview with Chambers didn't last more than twenty minutes. There wasn't even enough time for my brew to go cold. Short as the interview was, it was fruitful. Chambers must have thought he was a super-grass or the like, demanding to be placed in a safe house and guarded 24/7. I told him where we were putting him was the safest place in the city. He liked that, he just didn't know it was to be in segregation on the remand wing at Hull Prison.

Once we convinced him he would be safe until the case concluded, he "sang like a canary" as the say in the gangster movies. Although Chambers was only a small fish and not privy to the important stuff, he did fill in a few gaps. We had a name, one that had been coming up more and more in the last few days: John Shaw. Not only was this Shaw bloke responsible for running a number of illegal massage parlours-cum-brothels about the city, he was well and truly in the frame for the illegal importation and selling-on of girls from eastern Europe. I asked Chambers if he'd come across Reeta, Kaja's sister, he reckoned he didn't know her, but said if she wasn't dead then there was a good chance she'd been moved on to Newcastle, Shaw was starting to do a lot of business up there.

Funnily enough, Chambers had a clean sheet—the only thing we would be able to charge him with was fly tipping. I know he'd been setting fire to a vehicle that was connected to a serious crime, but there was bugger all else to charge him with, and he was likely to get away with community service. But I didn't tell him that when I had him taken to Hull Prison, all for his own protection of course.

I did a bit of serious thinking, and decided regardless of the position with the Serious Crime people; if this Shaw bloke could lead me to Osbourne then I was going to have the bastard. But first I wanted the bloke who'd broken into my car, Darren Taylor.

***

Phones were ringing, computers buzzing and printers churning out paper; it made a change to see and hear everyone hard at it. I walked to the far end of the room and tried to make some sense of the array of mind boggling information on the whiteboard.

'Thanks very muchly,' I said, Ria had brought me a brew. 'What do you reckon?' I added, nodding towards the display.

She picked up a felt pen and started to scribble. 'Number one, Olga Insk, eastern European, found dead in the snow.'

'Not to mention she been dead for quite a while before the body was dumped.'

'Two, someone tried to frame you for her murder.'

'That raises the question why? Have we managed to trace the little shit who broke into my car?'

'Taylor. We did manage to get an address but it looks like he's gone to ground. The neighbours said they haven't seen him for days. And number three, Kaja's sister Reeta goes missing.'

'From what Roose said, she could well have been sold on to this Newcastle outfit. Get Steevo to see if there's any progress with Newcastle CID.' I sipped my tea and thought I'd lighten things up a bit. 'Did you make this? You usually make a decent brew. This is like p—' She didn't let me finish. I smiled to myself: so easy to wind up, she didn't even turn around and insult me, just carried on.

'Four, attempted murder on Kaja.'

'Well, we know Chambers is out of the running, but this Shaw bloke seems like an odds-on favourite for it. Well, what does it tell us?'

'It seems to me that Serious Crime are far too interested in the small fries on our patch.'

'Patch, you sound like you're on *The Bill*!'

'Don't get sarky. As I was saying, they're sticking their noses into our business, so let's stick our neck out and follow up anything we've got on Shaw. If he can lead us to Osbourne, I don't see we have any other choice but to pack up and forget about it.'

Ria's outburst, which was slightly out of character to say the least, brought Questy back to life. He came across and parked his arse on a corner of Wales's desk. I noticed Samantha shifting in her seat, not sure whether to join him at the front or not. I still hadn't quite made my mind up about her. I made a mental note to ask Ria what her opinion was.

'What's your thoughts then, Mike?'

'Simple, if Shaw can lead us to Osbourne, then I agree with Ria.'

'That's it then, we go after Shaw. Right, Mike, I want to run something past you.'

***

'Bloody hell, "H", it's a hell of a risk, we'll both be for the chop if this goes tits up.' I knew the DCI wouldn't be too keen on my proposal, but in the light of things—mainly me being put on the rack—I thought at a pinch he might go for it. The quick version of what I had in mind was this: to release the Russian and put surveillance on him. Yes, I know that Alexei had a good level of English but he didn't grasp the finer points of English Law. The plan was to release him with a caution.

Questy's bloke, William, was to help, I'd had a word with him and he agreed to go with the plan as long as it didn't compromise his legal standing. William was to replace Alexei's current appointed brief, and point out some non-existent technicality in his arrest—and bingo, the Russian would think we were a useless set of buggers, laugh his socks off and walk away.

And that was exactly what happened: as soon as he left the station, we had a tail on him, DC Russ Stevens, he's the most experienced DC on the team, and on top of that a good friend.

Chapter 16
The Gangster And His Friend

The way things were going I was far from pleased, and for once it was good to be kept in the loop, the police loop. My contact, or I should say acquaintance, at the Braemar Street nick, was unknowingly keeping me up to date with developments. Ok, so things didn't work out framing Blackburn, but what the hell? There was always another time.

It seemed my little *tête à tête* with Kaja had gone tits up as well. The girl was a hard one to put down; I'd have put my money on her being brown bread. The question now was, would she eventually come around—and if so, would she open her gob and drop me in the shit? I put my money on the latter, unless I could use her sister Reeta as an incentive. I could be very persuasive when I put my mind to it.

Bad news about Chambers getting nicked, then again what did I expect? Who the hell but a full-blown idiot would set fire to a car where there was bound to be plenty of CCTV? Outside of the KC Stadium I ask you! I'd heard he'd looked after his fat arse and put my name in the frame. Well, I can tell you one thing for free: whether he went down the road or not, he was a dead man walking.

My new acquaintance paid me a visit. We were at my apartment on the Hessle Haven and as we all have to do now and again, she paid a visit to you know where. Now, I'm not one to miss an opportunity so I went through her handbag. Oh! Oh lo and behold I found her ID. She'd been telling porkies, she told me she was a civil servant—and well I suppose she was really—but she never told me she was a Customs Officer attached to the YPSIU, Yorkshire Ports Serious Incidents Unit, Blackburn's outfit. Well as you can imagine, we became best friends—you could even say it was a sleeping partnership. Here's to a long-lasting relationship.

Chapter 17
The Policeman Goes Solo

No sooner had Russ left the station hot on the trail, as they say, Alexei was dialling on his mobile. When we'd checked it, there were numerous calls to one number in particular, it turned out to be a non-registered pay-as-you-go mobile, not a cat in hell's chance of tracing it. Didn't take an idiot to guess that it belonged to Shaw.

Since we'd raided the house down Coltman Street, Alexei was, for want of a better word, homeless. Russ followed him on foot to a house down St. George's Road. He knocked and a young woman let him in. The address was checked out on the database but it didn't throw out any interesting information: it wasn't known to us.

I'd told Steve Wales to go and get his head down for a few hours. He wasn't pleased, in fact he was extremely pissed off, when I told him he was taking over surveillance when Russ knocked off. Russ duly found a secluded spot and kept his eye on the Russian for the rest of the day. Nothing happened.

Steevo might have had a go about having to do night surveillance, but he always did a good job. At least he had a vehicle to keep warm in as the temperature dropped. I grabbed a sandwich and ate at my desk while I caught up a bit on the neglected paperwork; there was nothing to rush home to, after all. After a couple of hours I'd had enough, so decided to pay Steevo a visit. I drove down St. George's and parked a fair way from the pool car, fastened up my coat, left my car and started to walk towards Steve. As I got nearer, I could have sworn he looked as if he was asleep, head laid back on the headrest and mouth wide open, I banged on the roof with flat of my hand and climbed in.

'Nodding off, Steve?'

'Nah, just resting my eyes.'

'Ok, you've convinced me. What have you got to tell me?'

'Not a lot, he hasn't left the house since he arrived. Would it surprise you if I told you there has been a steady stream of blokes going in and out?'

'Punters?'

'It seems we have another house of ill-repute.'

I wondered why this hadn't shown up on any intelligence reports; curious. I gave Steve a nudge when I saw the front door of the house open. It was our man.

'Hey up, looks like he's on the move. Come on, let's get some fresh air and see where the bugger is going.' We followed at a discreet distance up St George's onto Hessle Road. He was going to the pub. He went into the *Halfway*, so did we. The *Halfway* is one of the few remaining old fishermen's pubs. In the 1960s and 70s it would have been packed with *three day millionaires,* the name given to the fishermen who, after three weeks on board a trawler working their guts off, would return home to blow their wages inside seventy-two hours and then go back to sea.

I found a corner table away from the bar with a good view of what was going on, while Steve went to get the drinks in. It was fortunate that he wasn't known to Alexei.   He came back and put a glass of Coke down in front of me.

'What's this?' I asked, giving him a disgusted look.

'Aren't you driving?' The insubordinate sod said, smiling.

'Fair point.' What else could I say? I sipped. 'Is he talking to anybody?'

'No, but he keeps looking at his watch.'

'Right, we'll hang about and see what comes up.' I took another sip of the drink. 'Steve, I can't drink this fizzy stuff. Go and get us a couple of pints. Nobody on Hessle Road drinks Coke.' I gave him a fiver. 'Much better,' I said when he returned with two pints of Best Bitter, I took a swallow. 'Our boy still watching the clock?'

'Not for much longer.' He nodded across the bar. A bloke, who looked too smart for this part of the city, had come in and made a beeline for the Russian. He was about five ten, maybe six feet tall, cropped hair with a good tan that didn't have the orange sun-bed tinge.

'What do you reckon? Shaw?'

'I'd put my wages on it, boss.'

I was thinking he might be right. 'Looks like they're having words.'

'Not a happy bunny, is he?'

Alexei looked agitated, to put it mildly.

'Are we picking him up?' Steve asked me.

'We should, but it would be good to see where he might lead us.' Our cars were too far away to follow if he decided to make a quick exit. I took out my mobile and called the nick, I wanted an unmarked vehicle outside ASAP to follow him. 'Right Steve, here's what we'll do. There should be a car outside in a couple of minutes, I'll take the smart fella, you stay with the Russian shit bag. Let me know if anything happens.'

I swallowed down my pint and went outside, an unmarked car was ready and waiting. I thought it only fair that Ria should be in on this, so I gave her a call on the mobile to come and join the fun. She must have broken every speed limit between her home in the east of the city and my location, as she was there inside ten minutes. I swapped cars and told my driver to get himself back to the station.

'What kept you, get stopped at the lights?' Can't beat a bit of sarcasm to wind her up.

'Don't start , "H", you're lucky I'm here at all.'

'Why? You don't have a social life.'

'I was just thinking about getting a shower, then I wouldn't have heard the phone and I wouldn't be here.'

'Never mind, you can get one later.' I made a pretence of wrinkling my nose as if she ponged.

'Cheeky git! Is that him?'

The bloke I was hoping was Shaw walked out of the pub. A private hire car pulled in as he did and Shaw climbed in beside the driver. Alexei stayed inside the pub.

'Follow that car!' At least she smiled.

Down St. George's Road, Anlaby Road, Chanterlands Avenue, he cut through Goddard Avenue, then turned left

135

into Newland Avenue and pulled up. He paid off the driver, walked across the road, fumbled in his pocket and took out some car keys, then climbed into a shiny black BMW. He only drove it two hundred metres or so and pulled up, so we did the same.

'What was that all about?'

She just shrugged. 'Looks like he's waiting for someone.'

'We'll make a detective of you yet,' I told her. All I got was one of those contemptuous looks, I'm used to them. We sat watching for about five minutes.

'Are my eyes deceiving me?' she asked.

'No they're bloody not. This I cannot believe.' I sat there with my mouth wide open.

'For Christ's sake, "H" what's going on?'

'I haven't got a bloody clue.' As I said, it was pretty obvious he was waiting for someone, the trouble was *who* he'd been waiting for: it was our Customs and Excise Liaison Officer, Sam-who-likes-to-be-called-bloody-Samantha, and she was getting into his car. We watched as she got into the passenger seat, leaned across and gave him a peck on the cheek.

'What on earth does Samantha think she's doing, getting into a car with a gangster?' Ria was as dumbfounded as I was.

'Hang on a minute,' I said to her. 'To be fair, we didn't know ourselves it was Shaw until half an hour ago. And might I add, we still don't know for certain, it might be completely harmless.'

'Oh yeah and pigs might fly.'

'Look they're moving, let's go.'

I hoped to God that all was not what it seemed. We followed them to Mr. Chu's Chinese Restaurant on St. Andrew's Quay Retail Park, said to be the largest Chinese restaurant in the country and a big favourite of the ex-Deputy Prime Minister, John Prescott, I've been there myself but I'm not a big lover of Chinese food.

It looked as if they were going to be in there for some time, so there was little point in hanging about all night. I thought I'd give it an hour or so and come back. Ria was wanting her shower and my stomach thought my throat had been cut, so she dropped me back at my car and headed off, while I bought some dubious burger and ate in my car.

I finished my meagre supper and found myself heading for the Hull Royal to check on Kaja. Stable, the nurse told me. They were going to try to bring her out of the induced coma the following day. I was keeping everything crossed.

After the stifling heat of the hospital, however, I felt frozen through by the time I got back to my car. The heat when I started the engine was bliss. It was only thirty minutes since I'd left them at the restaurant, time for me to take another trip to Mr Chu's.

Shaw's car glistened with frost, and it was still parked up in the same spot. The car park was busy but spaces were available, so I slid the car—literally—in-between two other vehicles, and kept the engine running so I didn't freeze my balls off. A good tip an old CID Officer had taught me was to always keep a camera in the glove box, you never know when it might come in handy, and it was a habit I'd taken to early in my career. The trouble is nine times out of ten the camera battery will usually be flat when the time comes to use it.

Through the steaming up windscreen, I had a good view of the restaurant entrance. I double checked the camera and thankfully the batteries still had life in them. I turned the car blower onto full while I sat watching for Samantha to come out with her bloke. After an hour or so, I was busting for a pee and was contemplating doing it behind the car when I saw them coming. Oh bugger, the pee would have wait. I watched as they neared the vehicle and pointed my camera through the glass, click, click. I snapped a few good head shots before they got in the car, then it was back on the road.

They didn't head back to Sam's place on Newland Ave, but further west of the city towards Hessle. Traffic was almost non-existent: the majority of the cars on the road were taxis. I knew this Shaw bloke wasn't a numpty so I kept two vehicles behind them and they finally stopped outside a modern apartment complex at Hessle Haven, right on the river front facing the Humber. I pulled into a parking space with no problem and watched them go in. It looked as if Samantha had had one over the odds by the way she wobbled on her heels and clung on to him. Only two minutes later, the light came on in a second floor window and then the curtains closed. I sat and watched for forty minutes or so, but they looked to be settled for the night. By then I'd had enough myself and took a slippery drive on the frosty road back to my apartment on the marina.

After a hot drink with a decent noggin of rum in it, I felt more than weary and then it was time for a wash. The shower could wait until the morning: I just couldn't be arsed tonight. My body told me I needed sleep, but my head wasn't having any of it.

Chapter 18
The Gangster Gets Some News

I couldn't believe my ears when I heard Alexei's voice on the disposable mobile; how the fuck had he managed to walk? I would have bet my pension on not seeing him again for a good few years, yet here the wanker was, giving me a bell. I had a dinner date later in the evening and didn't want to fuck about so I arranged to meet him in the *Halfway* on Hessle Road. Oh for fuck's sake, did I feel overdressed when I walked in: everyone seemed to be in jeans and hoodies and here was I dressed up in Armani gear. I stood out like a spare prick.

The Russian was already there when I arrived, and stood propping up the bar with a pint in front of him. I got some strange "what the fuck is he doing here" looks as I went to join him. I didn't speak, just nodded to the barman, gave him a fiver and ordered a whiskey; he put my drink and change down and sauntered off to serve some scruffy shit at the other end of the bar.

'How the hell did you get out?' I asked. Alexei gave me a grin, shrugged his shoulders and went into an excited tirade of broken English. Eventually I managed to get him to slow down, and he told me the story of how he'd been appointed a new brief who'd found a loophole in his arrest, some cock and bull story about a technicality. Technicality my arse, there was definitely something a bit fishy about his tale. I told him he was a gullible tosser and that I was no way convinced by what he told me. I took his phone from him, deleted my mobile number and told him not to contact me again. If I wanted him, I'd find him. I ordered another whiskey and knocked it straight back. The more I thought about it, the more I thought something was dodgy.

I glanced at my watch; I was running a bit late, I hadn't planned for the impromptu meeting with Alexei, and my dinner date with my Customs Officer beckoned. Samantha was peeking through her living room curtains as I drove up, and came out as soon as I pulled in outside her house on Newland Avenue. A quick hello, then we headed off to Mr Chu's Chinese Restaurant. I've heard John Prescott and his wife Pauline had even entertained Tony Blair there; apparently the Prescotts go there three or four time a week. I shouldn't knock the bloke, he did a lot for the Hull fishing industry in the old days.

Samantha was very forthcoming with the conversation during our meal; it must have been due to the best part of a bottle and half of Zinfandel she'd drunk. After I figured she'd been plied with enough vino to seriously cause concern to her liver, I casually turned the conversation. Just like the wartime saying: "Loose Talk Costs Lives."

'The way you've attacked the wine, I guess you've had a bad day.'

'Bad day! You don't know the half of it. The longer the day went on, it just got worse, there's all sorts of interesting stuff going on and my boss seems to be keeping me on the sidelines. It's not fair. I want to be involved in the important stuff.'

'Like what?' Why not ask, she seemed to be getting things off her chest.

'Oh you know that case I mentioned, girls imported illegally for prostitution? This looked like it was going to be interesting stuff. Well they've only gone and released the Russian we arrested, hoping he will lead them to someone called Shaw. I mean, criminals all over the place and I'm not even getting a look-in.' She was really going for it. 'I did tell you I work with the police, right?' No, she hadn't. 'Well I'm supposed to be the liaison between the Customs agencies and the police for God's sake.' She hardly paused for breath, when she did she went for the wine bottle and topped up her glass, and I placed my hand over my own glass.

She was well on the way to being stoned, but I managed to get her to the car in one piece without her sliding on her arse and we went back to my place. The major problem I was facing, was if they were already tailing the Russian when I'd met him in the pub, there was a good chance they were onto me and Samantha.

You know, in other circumstances Samantha was the kind of woman I'd like to get to know further, maybe even have a proper relationship with—I cannot believe I just said that, it could damage my credibility. As it was, I decided this was going to be our last night together.

We made drunken love; well Samantha did, it lasted all of five minutes before she fell asleep, snoring like a trooper. She didn't move a muscle as I got out of bed, walked across and moved the curtains aside and looked out; Nothing, just dark, cold and frosty. She didn't stir as I dressed. I went downstairs and had a coffee while pondering over what my next move should be.

Chapter 19
The Policeman Doubts Himself

Life was good and I was almost drooling at the thought of a bacon banjo. I thought it best to let Ria and Questy know where I was, so phoned across to the squad room to tell them they could find me in the canteen. Hell fire, my bloody shoes were at it again: squeak, squeak. I tried walking on my toes but that only made me walk with a camp mince. It's got to the point of mortification: people look around and smile, but I try to ignore them. Bloody shoes.

When I reached the counter there was no-one there; I thought the young Goth girl would be in the back. I gave her a couple of minutes, then leaned forward on the counter and shouted.

'You there, Jenna?'

'No you'll have to make do with me,' a voice called back, it was Bren.

'Bren, it's good to have you back.' I still think maybe we could have had a good thing going if it wasn't for unfortunate circumstances keeping us apart. Maybe one day …but it was probably too late.

'Well it's not good to be back.'

'You been under the weather or something?'

'No, just had a couple of days at my sister's. What can I get you?'

I really wanted the bacon sarnie. 'Just a slice of toast and a fresh orange, please.' I'd felt crap, all sudden like.

'Harry? Harry'

I heard Bren call after me but I carried on walking. Stupid, I know, but I couldn't remember if I'd taken my medication—I'd had one too many of these episodes lately. I found myself in the car-park smoking shed, I seemed to lose control of my hands, it wasn't the cold, they just wouldn't stop bloody shaking. It took me three attempts to light my fag. Things didn't improve as I sat in the plastic bus shelter freezing my knackers off, I felt fuzzy headed as if I was half pissed. Thinking back to the other day in the car when I'd had that episode and the other—what can I call them—happenings? I suppose it's as good a word as any. It had to be my medication not agreeing with me. My smoking was back to the level it had been before I was hospitalised, and two cigarettes later my head cleared a bit. At first I was a bit shaky on my pins when I stood up, so I put out a hand on the cold plastic sheet to steady myself and eventually felt ok enough to take a steady walk across to CID.

'Come on, Harry,' I said to myself. *'Pull your fucking self together.'* Grabbed the door handle with a cold, sweaty hand, so far so good. Fixed smile on face, ok. Opened door and walked in. I nodded to a couple of the team. I didn't trust my mouth to say anything coherent yet. I shut myself in the office until I felt more like my normal self: *normal,* for fuck's sake.

After a while I thought I'd best make an appearance, and besides, I was interested to know if Steevo had anything to report from the previous evening, but first I was going to drop my camera off with Tosh, the CSE, and get him to print off the pictures I'd taken outside Mr Chu's. By the time I got back to the squad room I was feeling marginally better. I put on my best piss-taking face and started with the usual, as Ria would expect it.

'Good morning, Sergeant. Not making a brew are you?' Ria gave me the raised eyebrows. 'Never mind, Steevo will do the honours, won't you DC Wales?' Yet another disgusted look. 'Bring 'em through, Steve, and we can do a catch-up.'

Ria followed me through to my office. 'Well that was a bit of a turn-up for the books last night,' she said.

'And wait 'til I tell you the rest! Ah, cheers, Steve, pull up a pew,' I told him when he passed me my mug. 'Right, you first, Steve. Anything happen after I left the pub?'

Steevo shuffled in his seat. 'The Russian seemed to have a bit of a slanging match with the bloke in the suit, there was a fair bit of fingers poking chests and then the suit left. Alexei stayed a while longer and had another couple of pints then buggered off.'

'Did he talk to anyone else?'

'Only the bloke behind the bar. I followed him back to the house down St. George's, and sat in the car for a while keeping an eye on things until my balls started to freeze, but he never surfaced again. In other words, absolutely zilch.'

'Was it an *open* eye?'

'Boss, I'm hurt you should doubt me!' I smiled. 'I came back to the station and signed out and had uniform to do a half-hourly drive past.'

'What time did you knock off?'

'Just after midnight.' He'd stayed the course.

'Is Samantha in?' Ria asked him.

'Don't know, want me to check?'

I said yes and gave Ria a look.

Thirty seconds later he was back. 'Not in yet, Boss,' he said, poking his head around the office door.

'Cheers, Steve. Will you ask DS Quest to come in?'

'What can I do for you, "H"?' Questy said as he came in and parked himself.

'Samantha,' I said. 'Is she usually late?'

'No, it's not like her. She must be stuck in traffic or something.'

Before the conversation went any further, Tosh, the CSE, knocked and pushed the office door open. 'Room for a little 'un?' His standard greeting. 'The snaps you took,' he said, dropping a folder on my desk, 'need anything else?'

I said no, thanked him and he left. I opened the folder, took out the blown-up prints and spread them out on the desk. Both Ria and Questy leaned across to get a closer look.

'What on earth are we doing with surveillance pictures of Samantha?' It was as if Questy was challenging me.

'Strictly speaking, Samantha wasn't the focus of the pictures. It's the bloke with her, we believe him to be Shaw.'

'If it's Shaw, what the hell is Samantha doing with him?'

'That Mike, is the question Ria and myself have been asking ourselves.' I went on to describe last night's surveillance in detail, right up to them going back to the apartment in Hessle.

Questy was seriously put out. 'There's got to be some simple explanation …' He let the sentence hang as I held up my hand. I picked up the phone, aware of Mike's eyes boring into me: seems he and Samantha had grown close in the short time she'd been with us. I keyed in a number.

'Steve,' I said into the handset, 'Samantha turned up yet?... No?... Has she rung in?' Another no. 'Mike, get yourself around to her house, take Steve with you.' He didn't need telling twice, he was off like a flash.

I had other plans, organising a trip to Hessle Haven. This time I was going mob-handed. If this bloke was Shaw, I wasn't going to take any chances. Ria liaised with uniform and sorted a van full of task force officers, the heavy gang.

Questy gave a call when they'd got to Samantha's house. There was no sign of her. Steve Wales had carried out a bit of discreet breaking and entering around the back. I told him I didn't want to know about it. From what they could make out, it didn't look as if she had been home since she left the previous evening. I told Questy to meet us at Hessle.

If Shaw and Samantha were in the apartment, the last thing I wanted to do was spook them so we did the softly, softly approach, no blues and twos. I wasn't sure if there was a rear door or not, but there was bound to be some kind of fire exit so I sent some of the lads around the back, just in case. The rest of the team were to stay in the unmarked van until we gained access to the premises. Questy and Steevo drove up as we were getting ready to make our move. I glanced across, but Mike just shook his head. With my back towards the river, the wind fair cut through my heavy coat. I stood on the pavement looking up at the second floor window: the curtains were still shut. I had an ominous feeling about it all but did my best to shake myself out of it. There wouldn't be any problem gaining entry, just ring a couple of bells, show some ID and we'd be in.

The front door was duly buzzed open; an old chap stuck his head around his door, Ria flashed her warrant card at him and told him to go back inside and keep his door locked. He soon scampered away when he saw the lads alighting from the van. Easy does it, quietly we climbed the stairs, doing our best not to make too much noise on our way. I tried the civilised approach first and knocked at the door. No answer, so I knocked again, louder this time. Still no response, so just on the off chance, I tried the door. It was locked.

I nodded towards one of the big lads, the one with the steel door enforcer, and then moved to one side. He was already sweating in his riot gear as he came forward, he took a deep breath and I could see him counting to three, then he swung the steel ram at the door lock. Bang! Crash! The wood splintered into pieces and the door swung inward on its hinges. Still no sign of life from inside.

I stood on the genuine oak-board flooring, copper's boots scuffed the polished surface off as they rushed past me.

'Kitchen clear,' I heard someone shout, followed by numerous "clears" as the place was checked, then I heard.

'Boss, in here.' It came from the bedroom, it was Questy. The uniform team started to make their exit once the apartment was confirmed as safe. I went through. I won't bore you with the description of the bedroom, we all have one, all I will say is it was very, very luxurious. Questy had turned the light on, Ria walked across and opened the still closed curtains. All the time, Questy stood staring down at the bed, more precisely at the woman who lay on the bed covered with the duvet. He put his latex covered fingers to her neck, no pulse. Samantha was dead, stone cold dead.

What can I say? I was not the only one devastated by the sight of our dead colleague, Samantha. Mike, who'd gone an extreme shade of grey, made for the bathroom.

'This is not what I was expecting,' I mumbled out loud to no-one in particular. 'Clear the room.' No-one moved. 'Come on now, out!' I yelled, trying to jolt them out of it. 'Ria, get Tosh on the AirWaves, I want Crime Scenes here yesterday and you'd better call the duty FME.' Ridiculous I know, but we always need a doctor to confirm that life is extinct.

Ria disappeared through the door with a radio in her mitt, Steve Wales was pushing the remaining uniform out of the front door and trying to secure the scene until CSE arrived, Questy just stood there, staring through the bedroom doorway. I, in all honesty, just didn't know what to say to Mike, they had obviously grown a lot closer than I realised. I grabbed him by the elbow, walked him out of the bedroom and closed the door behind us. I told him to go and get some fresh air.

I could hear drawers and cupboards being opened in the other rooms, I hoped to Christ they didn't disturb too much before Tosh and his team arrived. I didn't have to worry: everything was gone, as if no-one had ever lived there. Puzzling, to say the least. 'You see this coming?' I asked Ria, who stood staring at the closed bedroom door. 'Ria?'

'No, it was the furthest thing from my thoughts.'

'We should—I should have done something last night and she'd still be alive.'

'Come on, "H", you know better than that. We didn't know the bastard was going to kill her.'

'Looks like the CSEs have turned up,' I said when I heard more vehicles pull up outside. I went to see how Questy was getting on. He was two hundred metres down the road, stood by a burger van at the river front viewing area. I pulled up my coat collar and went to join him. 'You alright?' He nodded. 'You don't look alright,' I told him.

'I'll be fine, "H", just the shock, I didn't expect…you know.'

'I know all fucking right! None of us expected this,' I said. 'Give us a coffee, mate,' I said to the bloke in the burger van. He poured hot water over instant coffee in a plastic cup, slopped in some milk and pushed it across. 'Cheers,' I said, pushing a pound coin across the counter.

'How come she was seeing Shaw?' Mike asked as he turned to face me.

'I'd put my money on it that she *didn't know* who he really was. I don't think she'd have knowingly been associated with a villain; on top of that we didn't have a clue ourselves who Shaw actually was until now.' We stood protected from the elements in the lee of the van, not saying anything: no words were necessary, we'd known each other a long time.

There was a sombre mood about the nick when we got back; as they say bad news always travels faster than good. Ok so Sam-who-used-to-like-to-be-called Samantha hadn't been with us very long, but nevertheless she was one of us, until proved otherwise. I sat, rocking back and forth in my chair nursing a cold brew, thinking about what I would say to her family, when the office door was pushed open. I was miles away and nearly spilt my tea down my shirt.

'Bloody hell, Russ, you know how to wake a bloke up.'

'Sorry, "H", I've got a bit of good news.'

'I could do with some,' I muttered, straightening my chair. 'Come on then, lift my spirits.' I put my cold mug down on the desk.

'It's Kaja, she's back in the land of the living.' Now this was good news. I'm ashamed to say I hadn't given her too much thought over the past twenty-four hours, what with everything that had developed.

'Fantastic news! Now that *is* better than a kick in the arse,' I said. 'Fancy a run out to the Infirmary?'

We went in my car, no police radio, all the better. Nice and quiet, only *Classic FM* on the radio. It took us longer to park the car than it did to get there. The place is notorious for lack of parking. I had been known to park in restricted areas before as some of you may recall. I don't suppose I should really knock the place, what with all the good they did and the lives they saved, but it's a horrible looking building: not very good on the eye.

I'd forgotten that we still had a uniform on sentry duty outside Kaja's room, so made a mental note to tell the duty Sergeant to have him called back. I couldn't see Shaw putting in an appearance now, way too risky. I told the uniform to go and find himself a cup of tea and we went in. It was good that Kaja had been moved out of Intensive Care. She was in a private room: it was a sight for sore eyes to see her sat up propped with pillows. She was still connected with wires and things that bleeped every couple of minutes; although obviously still tired, she looked remarkably well, all things considered.

This time I refrained from giving her a kiss on the cheek, I'd already had the piss taken out of me over the last time. Once the pleasantries were over, I asked about the night of her attack and she gave us chapter and verse, not that there was all that much to tell. She'd told the people in the refuge she was going to visit a friend, that friend turned out to be me. She saw the car parked a little way up the road but didn't take any notice, it all looked perfectly harmless. When the driver got out of the car he didn't arouse any suspicions. Once she reached where he was standing he turned around to face her, that was when she realised and started to panic but it was too late to try and run.

Kaja recognised her attacker, it was the same man who'd beaten her and thrown her out the night we'd had our *brief encounter.* The man we now knew as John Shaw. He never spoke to her, she saw the blade in his right hand, then he'd put his left arm around her and pulled her close as he thrust the knife into her stomach. She fell to the floor and watched as the vehicle drove away, end of story. I told her I'd visit again soon.

Tosh brought me the preliminary report on Shaw's apartment. The place had had a visit from the "cleaners", turned inside out, a professional job. The CSE gave me one of his famous unofficial, "in my opinion, but don't quote me" versions of his take of the crime scene. Samantha had been suffocated, probably with the pillow she lay on. Of course this couldn't be confirmed until the post-mortem had been carried out. As they say in the movies, the bodies were stacking up high and our squad had been depleted by one: now we were going to struggle. Ok, I knew I was the SIO, but as good as I thought I was, I still had to rely heavily on those around me and delegate, so I made a decision that wasn't going to win me votes in the popularity sweepstakes.

'Are you two coming for a brew?' Ria and Mike looked up over their desk dividers. 'I won't offer again,' I said and started to walk out of the squad room. It's like kids when you offer them sweets, I soon heard the patter of feet behind me. With all the activity going on in the station and the fact that my office was like a public right of way, the logical place for a quiet meeting was *Bab's Baps*.

Mike sat there with a face like a slapped arse. Ria grimaced as she wiped the tea rings off the table top with a tissue, what a state of affairs!

'Here we go,' I tried to sound brighter than they looked. I put the drinks down with a slop, making another mess for Ria to clean up. She just pulled a face. 'Right, I'm not going to mess about. Mike, I want you to take a couple of days off. Ria, you're acting SIO into Samantha's murder. Questions?' This was not what they'd been expecting.

'Time off, what the hell for?' Oh dear, I'd done it again.

'Not long-term, Mike. Like I said, just a couple of days to get your head together.'

'I don't need *to get my head together*, "H", I can still do my job.' He did that thing with the hair on his shirt collar.

'You're too close, end of. Decision made. Finish the shift and come back after the weekend.' I've known Questy for years and he can be a right stroppy bugger and hadn't changed a bit. He pushed back on his chair, stood up and marched out of the café without a by your leave. I was expecting a lot more resistance.

'What?' I said to Ria, who sat there throughout not saying a word.

'Nothing, I agree with you.' That was a turn-up for the books.

'Bloody hell, I thought you'd have been on his side?'

'He got pretty close, I think a couple of days away from the office might do him good.'

'My sentiments exactly.' It looked as if I might have got something right for a change. 'Are you ok with the Samantha thing? Say if you're not?' She didn't have any problems. We went back to the office. Things were on the up, about time too. Steve Wales was waiting like the eager beaver. Newcastle CID had come up trumps. The Geordie vice team had carried out a number of raids in and around Newcastle. It looked like Reeta had been found.

Chapter 20
The Gangster Cleans Up

Samantha had looked so peaceful when I'd gone back to the bedroom. She never budged an inch as I took the pillow from beneath her head and held it over her face. That just left the apartment to sort. The clean-up had gone according to plan, we *were* professionals after all. Clean up was an understatement: the place had been sanitised. There was nothing to connect me to the Hessle Haven apartment. My home of the past three years had been leased, furnished and the paperwork had been organised through one of our off-shore holding companies. The "cleaners" had removed every trace of me being there, except that is for the woman in my bed. Even that was stripped and changed and the contents put back. I'd stressed to them I didn't want Samantha ending up in a skip. Call me sentimental. It was a shame about Samantha, I really liked her company, but one has to be realistic about these things—self-preservation comes first. The rest of my personal stuff would be put in storage until it was needed.

I'd stuffed some things into an overnight bag, slung it into the boot of the BMW and driven off into the sunset, so to speak. I didn't go far, just a few miles up the road to the Hallmark Hotel. It's a nice place, I'd been to a wedding there a while back.

Up until yesterday evening, I'd been pretty sure the police didn't know who I actually was, but thanks to the stupid Russian, I wasn't quite so confident, which for me is unusual. I was convinced Alexei had been set up. There was no way the police would have let him walk. I mean, come on—keeping an illegal under- age girl captive! And they let him back on the street? I was no lawyer, but you had to admit it was more than a bit suss. It was time to make another phone call, Alexei knew too much.

Chapter 21
The Policeman Pays A Visit

When we knocked off for the day, I made a detour via the HRI. Kaja was making good progress, and she bucked up even more when I told her that Newcastle CID had found her sister and I'd made arrangement for her to be brought back to Hull. I had a word with the nurse in charge and she told me there was a good chance Kaja would be discharged in a couple of days. This was great news, but to be honest I was downhearted at the same time: it meant she would eventually be deported as an illegal immigrant. I had to look to the positive, though, she and her sister would be reunited with their family, but that would be after a lengthy trial. In the short term, I decided I'd help her and her sister find a place to live until it was all over. I'd be their supervisor, so there shouldn't be any bother with the courts wondering if they'd do a runner before the trial came up.

In the general frame of things, I wasn't overly thrilled with the way things were going. It was as if we had reached a stalemate. There was plenty of stuff going on but all the same we didn't appear to be making much headway. I couldn't see things improving until we got hold of Shaw. Alexei was our best option, it was time to pick up the Russian again and put a bit of pressure on. Between you and me, with what had happened to Samantha, I was beginning to think letting the Russian walk might not have been the good idea I thought it would be.

A restricted budget and such like had prevented us having constant surveillance on the house on St. George's Road, the place where the Russian was staying. I'd had to settle on uniform keeping a watching brief. As expected, the uniform log revealed that a steady stream of punters had been frequenting the place. The busiest time seemed to be between 10.30 p.m. and 2 a.m. If we were going to pick up Alexei, I wanted it to be when it would have maximum impact on the punters. I wasn't bothered about destroying the lives of the clients. They had made their bed, the choice was theirs: if they couldn't keep their brains in their pants, they deserved all that was coming to them, just like the other lot.

'Steevo!' I shouted, sticking my head around the office door. 'Got a nice little job for you.'

'Oh yeah? What would that be, Boss?' Suspicious bugger.

'Well, come in and I'll tell you.' I wanted him to keep surveillance on the house on St. George's Road. I particularly wanted to know if the Russian was at home.

'So what am I supposed to do about my tea?' He'd asked me when I'd finished.

'What about your tea?' I couldn't believe what I was hearing.

'Our lass will have it ready for me!'

'Steve, I do hope you are taking the piss.' I couldn't read him, his face was deadpan.

'Sorry, Boss, couldn't resist it.' The bugger sat chuckling in his seat.

'Twat, and there's me thinking you don't have a sense of humour. Get yourself some bloody sandwiches from the canteen and take a Thermos flask. You can always piss in it when you've finished the coffee. Get me on the mobile if you need me, I'm heading off home for a couple of hours.'

'Alright for some,' I heard him mutter as he left the office. Indeed it is alright for some, I told the rest of the team to do the same and be back at the nick for 9.30 p.m., moans and groans from nearly everyone. I told them to think of the overtime. I wanted to do this cock on by the book with no fuck ups.

***

It was brass monkey weather outside, and it didn't get any better when I eventually got home to the apartment: the central heating was on the blink and it was freezing. I rang the maintenance company, only to be told they wouldn't be able to get anyone here until the morning. I kept my coat on while I made myself a brew and sat back in my big chair. It wasn't long before my eyes started to close and I nodded off. All I saw was dead people floating in front of me, above me and below me. I'm not frightened of death any more, no need, it's a relatively peaceful occurrence, you know, like how grateful we are when a loved one or friend passes away in their sleep, bringing an end to suffering.

Tonight I was seeing death from a different perspective, not the peaceful one I'd already experienced. A large, open, white tiled room with steel operating tables that drip life's liquid into the drain gutters. I could smell formaldehyde, the coppery taste of blood bit at the back of my throat, making me want to retch. In front of me were bank upon bank of steel doors, autopsy room refrigerator doors, they opened in unison as I sat there in my chair. I could see violence, I could see souls seeking redress against those who had inflicted the pain, torture, suffering, and most of all I felt their sorrow and loss for those, who through no fault of their own, had to leave without being able to say goodbye.

Two hours later I was wakened to the sound of sleet drumming at the glass of the French windows. With the ghouls behind me, I had a quick shower and changed to freshen myself up a bit, then I sat at the kitchen table and had a coffee and a slice of toast. I could hear it was still siling down outside, beating against the windows. It was one of those evenings when you just want to sit by the fire with a good book, but muggins here had to go back to work.

***

I wasn't surprised when I saw Questy's Audi in the car park, but I was to be surprised by his manner. I walked across to his desk. 'I thought I told you to have a couple of days leave?' I said.

'I wasn't going to sit at home doing twiddling my thumbs when we've got all this going on, was I?' He said it with real attitude.

'You mean, "was I SIR". Office, now.' I wasn't having anyone speak to me like that in front of the team, not even Questy. I won't bother going into the details, but I gave him a right gob full and he went off sulking with his tail between his legs.

I calmed down by the time for the briefing in the canteen. It may have been closed but one of the uniformed lads made sure there was coffee and sandwiches in abundance. In a way, I was pleased Questy had turned up, the bugger. I could definitely use him on the raid, for all his stroppiness he is a bloody good copper. I made clear exactly what I wanted to happen, Questy and Russ, plus a couple of uniforms, would be in one vehicle, while myself, Ria and a couple of our lads would be in the second and a van with extra bodies in would keep out of the way until we gave them a shout.

We drove up to St. George's Road in quiet mode, no blaring horns or flashing lights. The task force heavy gang had been commandeered again, another blight on the overtime sheet. The transit full of big lads was to approach from the opposite direction, keep around two hundred metres away until a quick push on the AirWaves press-to-talk button and they'd approach post haste. We, on the other hand, had a good view of the house from where we were parked. There was nothing significant about the place to make it stand out from its neighbours: a three storey home with the obligatory satellite television dish and UPVC double glazing, the front doors opening straight out onto the street. Things looked all quiet. I got out of the vehicle and approached Steve Wales's pool car and climbed in beside him.

'What's going on then, Steve?'

'Bugger all, Boss, really quiet, only few punters in and out.'

'The Russian?'

'No sign. If he's in there, he's keeping his head down.' The door opened as we were speaking and another paying visitor left, the door closed behind him. I told Steve to stand by and went back to have a word with the team. It was time to move. I planned on doing exactly the same as we did on the previous raid, act like a pissed punter.

'Ok,' I said into the AirWaves. 'I'm moving, as soon as you see the front door open, move your arses. Don't forget, the main priority is the Russian.' I put the radio in my coat pocket, started walking with a bit of a stagger on and approached the house. So far so good. The icy pavement was like a sheet of glass and as I continued to stagger along, it took me all my time to keep my footing. Shit! I nearly went arse over tit as I reached the door. At least it made me look like a realistic drunk if anyone was watching my approach. I could imagine the lads sat in the cars laughing, wanting me to slip on my arse.

With one hand on the wall to keep myself from sliding down the pavement, I rang the bell. I didn't have to wait long before the door opened a crack and a face appeared.

'Yes, can I help you?' It was an English voice for a change.

'Hope so mate,' I said, smiling like an idiot. 'Know what I mean?' I pulled out my wallet and let him see the contents, so he smiled and opened the door wide. I wasn't going to charge in like I did on the previous raid, I'd learned my lesson with bruised ribs.

I could sense Steevo was coming up fast, so I did a quick sidestep just in time for the DC to burst past me and deal with the thug of a doorman. Steevo was closely followed by the heavy gang.

'Excuse me,' I said as I stepped over the doorman, who now lay face down on the floor with the knee of a uniform in the middle of his back, cuffing his hands behind him. Whoops, I'd accidentally given him a good kick as I passed. Someone had already opened the back door, there was a lot of shouting, screaming and blaspheming going on and Questy was coming towards me from the rear of the premises. A middle aged bloke wearing nothing but his boxer shorts and carrying the rest of his clothes bounded down the stairs, tripped, dived the last few steps and fell at my feet. It was childish I know, but I couldn't help but say, 'you're nicked,' as he lay there with shorts half way down his arse, showing the credit card slot.

Ria was one of the last to enter the house. I stood by the door. 'Yes, love, what can I do for you, looking for a job?' I said as she stood on the doorstep.

'Cheeky sod,' she said as she pushed past me and underpants man. Everyone was duly rounded up and put into one of the front rooms. It was a bit whiffy I can tell you, sweat and stuff intermingled with the girls' perfumes. I let the girls get some clothes on, but the punters…I made them stand to attention in their underwear. It appeared that all the personnel were accounted for except one: Alexei.

Compared to the house on Coltman Street, this one was an absolute palace, probably because the majority of the girls were UK Nationals with no tie-ins, who could pick and choose where and whom they worked for, within reason. The search began in earnest and produced a significant amount of coke, a few wraps of heroin and enough wacky baccy to send the entire population of West Hull loopy. We went through every room like a dose of salts, including the loft space and I'm pleased to say that we didn't find anything untoward up there. Unfortunately, the Russian was not hiding in the cupboard underneath the stairs. Was I worried? Me? Why should I worry? After all it was my neck on the line and I was the one who suggested we let him out. Shit.

'Questy, bring that turd of a doorman here, will you?' I said as I moved into the relative quiet of the kitchen. 'Sit down.'

He stood there, defiantly ignoring me. I'd nearly had enough. I put my face right into his, I could smell his manky breath.

'Sit down before I bloody knock you down,' I said, pushing him towards the kitchen chairs. I sat opposite. Questy had gone through the bloke's pockets and found some ID. According to his driving licence he was James Longthorne. He lived on the Orchard Park Estate.

'Before we cart you off to the nick, I have one or two questions for you Mr Longthorne.'

'You can ask, but it don't mean I'm gonna answer.'

'Alexei Pushkin, where is he?'

'Not here.' The cocky sod sat back, with his arms folded across his chest, staring up at the ceiling lights.

'I know he's not here, I want to know where he *is*.' The twat was really trying my patience. I didn't know why I let them get to me, after all these years you'd think I'd have been used to it.

'Well you'd better ask some fucker else, 'cos I *don't* know.' Oh, I was tempted, really tempted. If I hadn't had a badly bruised fist already, I'd have cracked the bugger good and proper. I know Questy would have turned the other way—again. 'Anyway, I 'aven't seen him for a couple of days.'

'He's been staying here?'

'Yeah, so?'

'So do you have any idea where he might be?'

'Not a fucking clue, like I said 'e 'asn't been around for a couple of days. I'm his mate, not his fucking mother, I didn't ask him where he was going *or* what time he'd be back.'

There was very little I could say to that. I hoped, but very much doubted, we might glean some more information once we got him back to the station. I *did* let the punters get dressed, once we got them back there. You could say they found it a little humiliating walking out to the squad cars in their underwear, carrying their clothes. They even got a few cheers from the lads back at the nick as they were trooped in.

The house was staffed with a mix of nationalities, three Eastern European, two Afro-Caribbean and five British girls. Of course the Eastern European girls were here illegally, but I wasn't sure if they were working against their will. They appeared quite happy with their lot. A big plus was that no-one was under age.

Further interrogation of Longthorne—sorry I meant to say interviewing of Longthorne—didn't give us too much that we didn't know already. Someone came around once a week to collect the cash and dole out the girls' wages. He didn't have a name for us but from the description it would be fair to assume it was Shaw. The same bloke was responsible for keeping the supply of drugs flowing. He wasn't going to be a happy chap when he found out another property had been put out of business, not to mention the seizing of the Eastern

159

European girls, who in a manner of speaking had been bought and paid for. But where the hell was Alexei Pushkin?

***

I didn't have to wait long for the answer to my question: he was found the next morning in a rubbish skip at the back of the Hull Ice Arena, stabbed and with his head caved in.

'Had your breakfast?' I asked Ria, who gave me a puzzled look at such a question.

'Yes, some scrambled eggs, why?'

'I don't want you bringing it back up when we go ice skating.'

'Ice skating?'

'Well no not exactly skating. Uniform have found the Russian, brown bread in a rubbish skip at the back of the ice arena. We're going to have a look.'

'Uh, nasty.'

Hull Ice Arena is just south of the city centre on one of those entertainment complexes with cinemas and restaurants, at the very busy junction of Castle Street. It didn't take long to get there, the car was just warming up when we had to get out. It was the usual scene as we drove up—with flashing blue lights and bobbies everywhere. The service area at the back of the arena was cordoned off with waist-high blue and white plastic tape printed with, "POLICE DO NOT CROSS".

It was pissing down so I fastened my jacket tight and put on my woolly hat, I didn't care if I looked a prat, as long as the piss-taking was done behind my back. We ducked underneath the tape and signed the uniformed officer's crime scene log, scrounged some protective suits and went over to where the CSEs were working.

'What do you reckon, Tosh?' I asked the lard arse of a Chief CSE.

'Can't say much ,"H", not until we get all this shit off him.'

I stood on a wooden pallet and looked over the side of the skip. He was right, the body was smothered in greasy bits of kebabs, food waste, burger wrappers and plastic coffee cups galore. But the aroma wasn't coming from the discarded rubbish. I didn't need a pathologist to tell me he'd been there for a couple of days, it was evident by the stink.

'Jump in and give him a hand,' I said to Ria, who didn't know if I was joking or not, then she twigged.

'Ha, bloody ha,' she said from behind the paper mask. 'Remind me to laugh.' I could make out the smiling eyes between the mask and the suit hood.

I left Ria watching while I went to the edge of the taped perimeter for a smoke. It was bloody cold, paper suits offer no extra thermal qualities whatsoever, so I stood smoking and kept cupping my hands around the cigarette until I saw them lift the body out. The trouble was, it was one of those high sided skips and manhandling the bulking dead weight of a fat, dead Russian looked no easy feat. With a fair bit of blaspheming, they managed to strap the body on a stretcher and hoist him up and over the side.

'Be careful, don't drop him,' I shouted. I was politely told to fuck off by someone. Tosh was puffing and panting like a good 'un by the time the body was laid on plastic sheeting.

'Well done, lads,' I said as I walked up, giving them a clap.

'Harry, you're a bastard,' lard arse said.

'You can't talk to me like that, I'm the SIO.' Perhaps I shouldn't have smiled when I saw him bend forward, rest his hands on his knees, gasping to get his breath back. 'One of these days you're going to be the one having the coronary, then what would you do?'

'Have three months on bloody sick leave like you did!' he panted out between breaths.

'Touché.'

There was no wonder they struggled; Alexei was a big bugger. The Russian was still covered in bits of greasy paper. His face looked in good nick for a dead bloke, but judging by the bloody fermenting stain on his chest, he'd well and truly been skewered with something bigger than a pocket knife. The post-mortem would tell us more, but to me the cause of death looked pretty damned obvious. I might add that I was pissed off to say the least: he might have been a lead to Osbourne. On top of that, I could see a bollocking coming before long.

***

Well, what can I say other than it was a crap start to an already crap day? Mind you, Steve Wales did brighten things up a bit when he told me uniform had found Shaw's car. Just by chance, a couple of the traffic lads who motor up and down the M62 and A63 in their jam sandwich had got caught short, one of them needed a piss. They pulled into the car park of the Hallmark Hotel, and lo and behold they'd noticed a nice shiny black BMW. It had been parked with the specific purpose of keeping it out of view of the main road. A PNC check revealed that the BMW was owned by Channel Holdings, the same company that held the lease on Shaw's flat.

I sent Steve Wales on a recce to check thing out at the hotel. Using a bit of Sherlock Holmes type deduction, we came to the elementary conclusion that the bloke booked into the room seventeen was our man. It had to be, the cheeky sod had booked in under the name of Harold Blackburn. It was in the back of my mind that if I was going to get a lead on my old adversary, Osbourne, Shaw was my best shot now that the Russian was out of the picture. So I decided to leave him be and have him put under twenty-four hour surveillance, bugger the budget. Don't worry, we fitted a tracker to his car. He wasn't going anywhere without us knowing.

Chapter 22
The Gangster Has A Visitor

I'd checked in at the Hallmark Hotel with no problems, but to be on the cautious side I parked the motor away from sight of the main road. I was only planning on staying a couple of days while I waited to see how things panned out. As you know, I'd already had to get in touch with my boss who was *not* best pleased with the way things had been going. In fact he was fucking furious and he told me to stay put.

Two hours later I got a call on my mobile. Not good news: the boss was coming to sort things out, just what I didn't want. I don't know what he thought he could do that I hadn't already. He'd booked an indirect flight from his home in Skiathos to Athens, then on to Amsterdam. This is where he was taking a risk, flying from Amsterdam direct into Humberside airport. It sounded way too risky if you ask me, but who am I to argue? After all he pays the wages.

I wasn't happy, but there was nothing I could do about it other than wait for the call, so I decided to take advantage of the hotel's facilities with a bit of R and R. As long as I didn't venture into the city, I reckoned I was pretty safe. The only thing that bothered me was the car. If you think back to when I met the Russian in the pub, I'd bet a pound to a pinch of shit that he was being tailed, so it seemed logical that so was I. And on top of that they must have found Samantha by now. Ok, the plods knew where I'd been living, but the "cleaners" were the best in the business, they wouldn't find a hair out of my head. My priority now was to have the same done to the car. One of the "cleaners" was on the way to sanitize the BMW. In other words, it was being sent to the crusher and someone was bringing a replacement vehicle. The R and R didn't last long: sixteen hours and thirty-five minutes to be precise 'til I got the call. It was time to pick Osbourne up. I drove my new vehicle, a VW Golf, out of the hotel towards the Humber Bridge and Humberside Airport at the same time the "cleaner" headed west on the A63 with the BMW.

It was an easy drive from the hotel to the airport. I parked up and had a casual wander into the terminal building, and everything seemed to be as it should, so I went back outside. Standing in the lee of the terminal building with yet another cigarette, I waited for the 9.30 a.m. flight from Amsterdam to arrive. The weather hadn't improved, it was still cold enough to freeze the balls off a brass monkey.

Humberside is a small regional airport within spitting distance of the east coast. A few flights head off to the sun but in the main, with only a single runway, it's one aircraft in and another out. The bread and butter runs are domestic flights and those to the near continent, nevertheless there is still the security to contend with.

I hoped the boss was prepared. I stayed outside, close to the building and waited. Two minutes early, the Amsterdam fight taxied up the runway. I wasn't going to take any chances with the airport security and waited outside the building until he'd cleared customs. He came out through the main doors, then stood and looked around, so I went across.

'Good to see you, John, it's been a fair while,' I said, as the boss approached, holding out my hand to shake only to be rebuffed.

'Well it's not fucking good to see you, what the hell have you been doing to my business?' He didn't give me a chance to open my mouth. 'You couldn't organise a fucking piss up in a brewery.'

This was going about as well as I expected. John Osbourne was not a man to be fucked with. There wasn't any point in trying to tell him it was just a chain of unfortunate events and that it wasn't my fault, the bloke wasn't interested in excuses. I kept my mouth shut and led him to the car. The journey back to the hotel was strained, to say the least, I was glad it was a short one: too many silences for my liking. I'd already booked him a room in the name of Van Uunsberne, an old family name apparently, something to do with his Dutch heritage. We dumped his bags and went for breakfast in the restaurant. The grilling began, and I don't mean the sausages.

Chapter 23
The Policeman Dines Out

There was a tap on the door and Ria stuck her head around the door frame. 'Technical Support have been on the blower, we have movement.'

'What sort, a bowel movement?' I just couldn't resist; no harm in being sarcastic now and again.

'You know, "H", sometimes, just sometimes I wish—'

'I know, what can I say?'

She just shook her head the way she does. 'Shaw, the tracker has kicked in, he's on the move.' At least she was smiling, even though the joke was rubbish, she's very polite.

'Which way is he heading? Into the city?' I asked.

'No, west along the A63 heading towards the M62, traffic has an unmarked car tailing him.'

'Ok, but we won't have long; once he reaches Goole he'll be off our patch. Get on to South Yorkshire to let them know we'll be poaching. I want him picked up before he reaches the A1.'

Communications had patched my AirWaves through to the traffic car doing the following so I could listen in to their running commentary, and one of the technical bods came and set my computer up so that I could follow the tracker. Bloody clever stuff—it was like watching one of those old video games, one blip following the other. Then something happened that I wasn't expecting. My guess would have been that he'd head south down the A1 towards London, or even for somewhere like Leeds to lose himself, but not our bloke. He turned off at South Cave, I was puzzled to where the hell he was going.

'Cheers,' I said as Ria put a brew down in front of me. 'I don't bloody believe it.' I said, then realised I must have sounded like Victor Meldrew off the telly.

'What don't you believe?' she said over my shoulder.

'Shaw. Why the bloody hell would he turn off at Cave?'

'Not a clue, Victor.' It made me smile. 'The front blip, that Shaw?'

'Yeah, the other's the traffic car keeping its distance.'

Ria pulled up a chair and we watched the cars go through Market Weighton and onto the York Road. According to the trackers they were doing a steady 58mph, just keeping inside the legal limit.

'He's turned off again.'

'I *am* watching, you know,' she said.

'Yes, but do you know where he's going?'

'McDonald's?'

'Good one, well I have a good idea.'

'What are you, "H", bloody clairvoyant? It's a blip on the screen and you know where it's heading, magic!'

'Oh ye of little faith.' I picked up the AirWaves and pressed the PPT to speak with the traffic officers tailing him. 'Blackburn. There's a scrapyard coming up on your left, about eight hundred metres, my best guess is that's where he's going. If I'm right and he drives into the yard, pick him up.'

On the screen you could see the traffic car picking up speed, then, when the BMW slowed, turned and stopped, our lads were right up his arse.

Then the AirWaves shouted at me. 'Sir, it's not him! It's not Shaw!'

'Shit, shit, shit!' I yelled. It was a good job it wasn't a conference call or I'd have been in for another bollocking. If it wasn't Shaw, who the hell was it? And where the hell was Shaw? To put it politely, I was what you could call pissed off with the way things were going or not going. It seemed for every step forward there was some bugger ready to knock us back another two.

While we were waiting for the driver of the BMW to be brought in, I decided the next rational step was a nicotine fix. I suppose you've noticed I was back to pre-heart attack smoking levels. The weather was still crap: freezing cold and sleety. I put my big coat on, made sure that my cigarettes were my pocket and paid a visit to the vending machine for a coffee of sorts. I told Questy to sort things out with the traffic lads when they

I didn't plan on being too long, it was too bloody cold. I made my way to the smoker's shed in the car park and sat on the bench. It was cold, I sat with my hands around the plastic cup staring through the Perspex panel. Then it happened again.

'So, things may be starting to happen,' I rolled my eyes back, I was talking to myself again. 'Give it a rest will you?' I said out loud to myself.

'Sorry Sir, did you say something?' Bugger, it was a uniform walking across the car park. I apologised, said I was miles away and just speaking out loud. The thing is, sometimes the voice does turn out some good ideas that are beneficial to the case. I know, I know, you'd think I was crackers talking to myself like that but it was not as bad as it used to be, it was the night terrors and the weird dreams that worried me.

Then it came again.

'Shaw and Osbourne, what are you going to do about them?'

I kept my voice low and talked into my coffee cup.

'Piss off, leave it to me will you,' I whispered.

'If I leave it to you we'll get nowhere.'

'"We?" I'm the detective, you're just a bloody voice inside my head. Why the hell won't you leave me alone?''

'Bad penny me, I always turn up.

Don't rise to it, Harry, I told myself, ignore it. I stood up, pulled the collar of my coat up, finished my coffee and put the plastic cup on the bench. I had intentions of a brisk walk around the block and then get back to work.

'Aren't you going to put that in the bin?'

"Keep your cool, ignore it." I thought.

'We haven't had a proper chat in quite a while.'

'I've already told you, SOD OFF, I can't be doing with this you're doing my head in.' I tried my best, I really did, but accepted I was in for some serious ear-bashing with myself, can you believe that?

'Go on then.' The up-shot of my schizophrenic conversation was, I decided, that I'd been too wrapped up in my own problems that I wasn't being diverse enough, thinking too laterally. It was now time to give myself a kick up the arse and thinking outside the box, as they say.

***

Giving myself a good talking-to seemed to do the trick, I felt on top form.

'I wondered where you'd got to,' Ria said as I walked in.

I smiled, she was used to me going on walkabout. 'Just a quick fag. Questy, round 'em up, let's see where we're at and if we can make any sense of this.,' I said as I entered the squad room.

Once we had everyone assembled, I stood in front of the whiteboards cluttered with photographs and notes.

'Did you get a hold of Tosh?' I asked Ria.

'Said he'd be along in a few minutes.'

I nodded. 'Mike, you had chance to have a word with the BMW driver?'

'Briefly, they've only just brought him in. One Curtis Palau, twenty-eight years old, with an address in Morley, Leeds. He's pleading ignorance and reckons he was doing a favour for a mate of a mate and just picking the car up take to the breakers.'

'Who's this mate?'

'Well that *is* a question, mate number one is John Smith, would you believe? And he doesn't know how to contact him. Mate number two is just a bloke in the pub who paid him cash in hand for the job.'

'Got room for a little 'un?' Little un! Tosh wobbled his lard arse down the squad room and sat down with his rather large rear overhanging the edges of a tubular chair.

'Tosh, what's the state with forensics?'

'Give me a minute to get settled, Inspector.'

'I'll give you bloody get settled, what have you got?'

'How long have we got?' I'm sure he was just taking the piss. 'I've had teams at both Samantha's house and the Hessle apartment. The forensic sweep of Samantha's place revealed nothing in the way of incriminating evidence, there was nothing to show other than a young professional woman living alone.'

'And that's it?'

'And that's it. The Hessle apartment was a different entity completely.'

'Go on.'

'The place was professionally cleaned.'

'I take you don't mean by Mrs Mop?'

'Hardly, when I say cleaned I mean sanitised. The place was almost sterile from what I could make out, every single trace of anyone living there had been removed.'

'You mean apart from Samantha.'

'There's no easy way to say it: even the body had been removed from the bed and bathed, the bedding changed and the body replaced in the bed.'

'Bloody hell, what was all that about?' I couldn't believe my ears. I know it's a cliché to say, but in all my years on the force it was the first time I'd ever come across anything like this. 'What about the post mortem?'

'Being performed as we speak.'

'Hazard a guess?' I asked.

'Unofficially, and don't quote me, but there were signs of petechial haemorrhages in her eyes and the neck area.'

'Come on, Tosh, what's that in my language?'

'There were small burst blood vessels in her eyes and the same thing was evident below the skin on her neck. I'd say she showed all the signs of asphyxiation, she was suffocated.'

'Cheers, another piece of the puzzle put into place.'

'Hang on a minute, don't take it as gospel, what with any trace of evidence being washed off the body. Combined with the fact the original bedding was removed, it's just an educated guess. Until we get the official PM report we don't know if we're on the money.'

'In that case thanks for bugger all, Tosh,' Questy said.

'I didn't say that I was finished, did I?' It was good to see him standing his corner. 'The body found in the skip, the Russian, is a different kettle of fish. I don't need a PM report to make a pretty damned good assumption as to cause of death.'

'That is?' I asked.

'He was beaten to death.' Tosh looked really smug.

'What about the stomach wound? You can't tell me that didn't have something to do with it?' That was Questy again, the cynical bugger.

'Actually it wasn't the cause of death. If you'd actually been there and seen what was in the skip you'd understand. There was a hell of a lot of building material in there, timber, angle iron and the like. As he was thrown in, it looked like he was skewered onto a length of timber.'

That shut the DS up. Steve Wales's mobile started singing out the theme from *The A-Team*, so he excused himself and walked to the far end of the squad room to take the call. After three minutes of animated conversation, he was beside me.

'That was Stella, the girl on the reception desk at the Hallmark Hotel. It seems Shaw never booked out.'

'Did anyone bother to make sure he'd checked out? Don't all speak at once.' Deathly quiet; it seemed he'd still been booked in there when we were chasing the BMW all over East Yorkshire. 'Right, Steve, you and Russ get down there and let me know what's going on. You never know, we might be able to salvage the situation.' It would be a bloody miracle if we could. Yes, I know I'm SIO and the responsibility lies with me, but hell, you'd have thought someone would have checked if he'd actually booked out.

It was nicotine, tea and more nicotine before I heard back from the lads at the Hallmark. I was trying to make some sense of the information on the white board when Questy gave me a shout, Steve was on the other end of the phone.

'Steevo, what have you got for me?'

'It seems not only is Shaw still a resident, he's gone and booked another room.'

'Any idea who for?'

'Russ is checking it out with reception now.'

'Anything else?'

'Hang on...Russ is on his way back.' I could hear mumbling at the other end of the line. 'Boss, are you sitting down?'

'Don't fuck about, Steve, spit it out.'

'The girl on reception said the room is booked out to a Van Uunsberne.'

'Sounds familiar. Have you had a look at him?'

'No, but from the description she gave, it sounds like your old mate.' He sounded somewhat excited.

'Which old mate would that be?' I didn't have a clue who he was talking about

'John Osbourne.' I let the line go quiet while it sank in. 'Boss, you still there?'

'Steve, if you're looking to go back in uniform you're going the right way about it. Put Russ on.' I thought I might get a bit more sense out of him.

'Sir?'

'What do you think, Russ? Is it Osbourne?'

'Can't say for certain, we haven't clocked him yet, but the description she gave is pretty close.'

'I want to know one way or the other, ok?' I hung up. There was all sort of crap going around in my head. I owed so much to John Osbourne: a near nervous breakdown, almost losing my job and a heart attack that nearly cost me my life. What a top bloke! I was going to enjoy getting the bastard this time, and make sure he went away for a long time.

Time went by slowly, and still there was no word from Steevo and Russ. Knowing DC Wales like I did, I'd put money on it that he was filling his boots at the bar and restaurant on expenses. Knocking-off time came and still they didn't have a positive ID on Osbourne. Ria was about ready to leave the office when I stopped her.

'Sergeant, what exciting plans have you for tonight, besides sitting bored out of your mind watching the television?'

'I suppose *you're* going to tell *me*?'

'How do you fancy a nice meal in a posh restaurant, on me?'

172

'How could a girl resist such an offer. The Hallmark?'

'Got it in one. Grab your coat, you've pulled!'

'Apparently that's a line my dad used to use.'

'Cheeky bugger. Ready?' I grabbed my coat.

***

The drive out to the *Hallmark* was horrendous, one lane blocked and the traffic crawled at snail's pace as commuters headed home.

'I hope you two are still sober,' I said as Ria and I walked into the bar.

'Boss, Sarge, we weren't expecting you. Can I get you a drink?'

I glanced at their glasses: good lads, they were on the soft stuff. Why not? In for a penny. I waved over the smart looking barman and ordered.

'Which room is he in?' Ria asked.

'Room fifteen, first floor. Shaw is in the next room. Apparently they have an adjoining door.'

'And you're sure he's still here?'

'Positive, Boss, the lift is on the blink so he has to come down that staircase. We can't miss him.'

I wandered over to the reception desk and showed a picture of Osbourne to the girl behind the desk. I got the confirmation that I wanted! I walked back to the bar beaming all over my face, I felt as if all my birthdays had come at once. There was just one more thing to do before we picked him up.

'Are we going in?' Russ asked as I came back.

'Soon, very soon. I got this pass swipe card from the girl, room fifteen next door, it's vacant. Go and stick your ear and a glass against the wall and see if you can hear anything.'

Russ trotted off, Ria got on the phone to see if she could muster a few more hands. Steve went to the gents and I went outside for a smoke, feeling well pleased with myself.

'We might as well go and have that meal I promised you. Those two can keep an eye on things, it doesn't look as if they're going anywhere,' I told Ria. 'We'll pick them both up when we're fed and watered and have a full team assembled. I'm not taking any chances with the buggers.'

We didn't pig out, we didn't have the time. I had some fancy fried fish with half a dozen chips stacked on my plate like building blocks, while Ria had a goat's cheese tart with a Greek salad. All washed down with a bottle of expensive sparkling mineral water. It was a pity we didn't have time for a starter and a pudding. All told, we were only in the restaurant for forty-five minutes. Russ had been keeping an eye on Osbourne's room, but there was still nothing to report; maybe they were in Shaw's room? I didn't know. Anyway, things stayed quiet. Steve kept an eye on the stairs while we went outside to check on the cavalry. I'd just lit up a cigarette when I heard sirens, a bloody patrol car was pulling into the car park, and there was me trying to keep things low profile. Shit, it couldn't have made any more noise! Someone was going to get their arse kicked.

Now it looked as if it we would have to get a shift on, half a dozen uniforms were tasked to take up their places near the fire escape. The four of us from CID, plus four PCs were going to make our entrance by the front doors of rooms seventeen and fifteen simultaneously. You know me by now, the plan was simplicity in itself: knock at the door, call out "housekeeping", and in we'd go. Failing that, we'd just use the master swipe card, but knowing the sort of dangerous people we were dealing with I preferred the softer option with less chance of anyone getting hurt.

Uniform were in place. We moved quietly along the first floor landing. My nerves were a bit shot, I can tell you. I'd been dreaming about this moment since before my heart attack. Outside room thirteen it was all quiet, Ria knocked on the door and called out: 'Housekeeping?'

No response, so she looked towards me. I was getting a good feeling so I told her to try again, knocking more assertively. Still no response. Everyone readied themselves as I took the card and passed it though the lock slot. Click, a push with my foot and I eased the door open.

EMPTY, no-one there. I opened the door to the adjoining room. No-one there either, what the hell was going on?

I stood in the middle of the room and looked around me. My head felt as if was spinning like in the film *Exorcist*. Then I heard Ria's voice as she took the lead.

'Steve, Russ check downstairs. You two,' she said to the uniforms. 'Check the public rooms on this landing.' Then she was on the AirWaves to the uniforms outside. 'They're not here, check the car park and the grounds.'

I eventually pulled myself together and nodded my thanks; not that they were needed, she knew how badly I wanted the sods. A quick recce of the rooms didn't give any clues: they hadn't taken anything with them, travel holdalls still on the floor, beds waiting to be made up and the stock of the mini bars well depleted. I was beginning to think maybe they were still on the premises. How the hell had they been able to leave the room without us seeing them, when the only access was from the stairs we'd been watching?'

A search of the hotel was being made for the pair, and Ria followed me outside when I went for a smoke. I think I bloody deserved one after this fiasco.

'Well, what do you think?' I put a fag between my lips and lit up.

'We had it all covered. They can't have left without passing us.'

'That's what I'd have reckoned, but it looks like they have done.' I got a few disgruntled looks from hotel guests as we stood in the hotel doorway with me puffing away. Then I heard heavy revs from a car and turned my head. A blue VW Golf pulled out from around the side of the building, heading to the main road. I recognised the driver as he showed me the finger. It was Osbourne.

Chapter 24
The Gangster And His Boss

We had breakfast in the hotel restaurant. Osbourne said he was knackered with all the travelling, so he decided we should meet up in his room after he'd got his head down for a couple of hours. "A couple of hours" turned into seven or eight and I'd enjoyed the respite.

It was early evening by the time he'd surfaced and we met in his room. He was half cut by the time I arrived, and started by giving me some serious ear bashing as he hammered the bottle of duty-free vodka. I wished he would steady up with it. He tends to get a bit more aggressive than normal when he hits the bottle and he's not the sort of bloke you tell he's had too much to drink. At times, it was difficult to understand him as the alcohol started to take a hold. His speech was barely coherent with the Geordie, Dutch gibberish, he reckoned it was something to do with his heritage as he always called you "man".

Osbourne calmed down a bit, and I was about to pick up the house phone and order room service, when there was an almighty racket outside, police sirens. Osbourne seemed to sober up immediately, I jumped up from my seat and looked out of the window.

'Cops have arrived,' it was as if he was expecting them.

'They had to arrive at some point, man.'

'Do you reckon they're looking for us?'

'Use your head, Johnny, who else have they come for? See that bloke down there, it's Blackburn.' Oh, I recognised him alright. 'Time to depart, got your car keys?' I nodded. 'Then follow me, man.' Funny, he was as sober as a judge, it made me wonder if the drunk stuff was all an act.

'Where are we going?'

'Home.'

'And where is home?'

'Anywhere you want it to be, Johnny boy.' He grabbed his travel bag, dug deep and took something out, I couldn't see what, but had a bloody good idea when tucked it into the waistband of his trousers.

I opened the room door and looked about. No-one in sight. He pushed me out of the way and took the lead, I followed him down the corridor. The corridor did a dog's leg turn to the left. There were doors on both sides, so we stopped at one signed "Staff Only". He banged on the door, no answer so he stood back, gave an almighty kick and the door flew inwards. It was the cleaner's room, once inside we piled a load of gear against the door to jam it shut. The window overlooked the side car park where I'd left the VW.

'Piece of piss, Johnny boy, nearly ground level,' he said to me as he opened the unlocked window and stuck his head out into the sleet. I put my head out of the window and looked: we were only one floor up but it was still long way to the fucking ground.

'Me first,' he said, and hoisted himself up onto the window ledge. That was when I saw the gun sticking out of the waistband of his trousers. He dropped over and down and landed like a cat. With not quite so much confidence, I followed, landing in a heap on the tarmac.

'That yours?' he asked, pointing towards the VW as we crouched against the wall with the sleet dripping off us. 'Well, let's go then. Give me the keys.'

Keeping as low as we could, we made a crouched run for the car.

'Where are we going?' I asked, when we were inside the vehicle.

'Told you, Johnny. Home.' I wished he wouldn't keep calling me Johnny.

Chapter 25
The Policeman Heads West

'You! Yes you!' I shouted to the driver of one of the traffic cars. 'Follow that car,' I said, as both Ria and I dived into the back seat. 'Call in the helicopter,' I told the driver's mate. As luck would have it, the chopper was already up and about, which was a good job because as we came to the A63 junction we didn't have a clue as to which way the Golf was heading. West away from the city towards the M62, North towards Beverley or over the Humber Bridge into Lincolnshire? We hung fire at the junction until the chopper was overhead and gave us directions. North, he was heading north up the A164 towards Beverley.

The A164 was a nightmare, roadworks everywhere while they converted it to a dual carriageway. The chopper had him in view. He was about half a mile ahead of us. Frustration was getting to me—so near, and now it looked like he might evade me once again.

'Put your foot down,' I told the driver.

'Right you are, sir.' He did as he was told; by hell did he start to motor. It was the drive from hell as we weaved in and out of traffic, we passed through red light single lane sections with cars flashing their lights and blaring their horns at us. I thought it might be Ria's turn to have a coronary. We managed to catch up a little when he turned west onto the A1079 towards Market Weighton and York, a decent road at last and we made some good progress. At that stage I couldn't think where he might be heading. Then I saw the sign for a place called Full Sutton and I knew.

Chapter 26

The Gangsters Go Home

He drove the VW out of the car park as if it was a Formula One car, straight across the path of oncoming vehicles. He fair scared me silly, he was laughing like he'd lost the plot.

'I do hope you've got a plan?' I said as we bounced around like a dodgem car.

'You ever been to Holland? 'Course you have, man.' The Geordie accent was creeping back in. Shit, we took out a line of traffic cones. 'Well, you're going again, Johnny.'

'This all part of the plan?'' His face looked like that of a madman.

'All part of the Great Escape, Johnny, Hollaaannndddd here we come.' He put his foot down harder on the gas to overtake three cars, it was a single carriageway with oncoming traffic for God's sake. I sat with my legs straight out stiff in the foot-well, grabbing the dash with my hands 'til my knuckles went white. I very much doubted we'd reach wherever we were going alive. I could hear what must have been the police helicopter overhead. I turned and looked out of the rear window. There was no sign of a pursuit car but I would have bet my last quid it wasn't far behind. We arrived alive, at a small private airfield at Full Sutton, not far from York. Osbourne drove straight past the security guard to an aircraft hangar at the far end of the field. It seemed the manic stage had passed and he was back in control of things. So this was it. A private plane to Holland.

I've never minded flying, but bloody hell, compared to what I'd been used to, the aircraft we were going to fly over the North Sea in looked like a toy.

'You all set for the big adventure, Johnny?' he asked me as he pulled the car up to a stop alongside the aircraft.

'If I don't want to end up in the nick, I don't have much say in the matter, do I?' I knew I wasn't looking forward to going on the run with a nut-job.

'Come on then, let's get out of this shit hole of a country, once and for all.'

'Not exactly how I would have put it...' I never got chance to finish.

'Get a move on.' I could hear distant sirens.

We climbed up the short ladder, I really didn't like the thought of being strapped into this narrow aluminium tube flying at two thousand feet. There looked to be half a dozen seats or so, but me and Osbourne were the only passengers. I got myself seated and strapped in, Osbourne took the co-pilot's seat. I pitied the pilot having to listen to him rant on while trying to concentrate.

'Okee doakee, let's go,' I heard him shouting to the pilot over the engine noise. We started to taxi out of the hangar and the bloody airfield floodlights came on, worse still I saw a stream of flashing blue lights. The cops had arrived.

'Come on, come on,' Osbourne was shouting and waving his arms about the small cockpit.

'Shit, what are we going to do now?' The lead squad car was gaining fast.

'Easy, Johnny boy.' Jesus, my heart flipped somersaults, he was holding the bleedin' gun.

Chapter 27
The Policeman Gets His Man

The airfield at Full Sutton was mainly used by the gliding fraternity and occasionally by privately-owned light aircraft. I kept looking at my watch, it had taken us the best part of fifty minutes to get to here, I only hoped we hadn't missed the bugger. A fleet of six squad cars ploughed through the gateway, I was in the lead car waving at the numbskull of a security guard to get out of the way before we flattened him.

I was surprised at how quiet it was. My driver pulled up alarmingly fast with a screech of brakes outside of the Nissen hut office. I leapt from the car and stuck my head around the doorway, but there was no bugger there. I gave a shout but no-one answered. The uniform in the vehicle leaned heavily on the horn, I turned to see what the commotion was all about and looked towards where he was pointing. My driver was a bit of an anorak when it came to aircraft, he told me it was a new 2011 Kodiak, eight-seater light aircraft. Its nose was edging out of a hangar at the far end of the field, and I just managed to get back in the car as he pulled away like a Formula One driver.

'Put your foot down.' I tried to stay calm.

'Right you are, sir.' Bloody hell, the G-force glued me to the back of the seat.

'I take it you've done this before,' I shouted at him above the revving engine.

'No, sir, first time.' Oh, hell, on we went as he opened the throttle, I wished I'd put my seat belt back on. The convoy followed suit, b-dump, b-dump as we raced along the concrete slab road. It was good to see someone had had enough sense to get the airfield floodlights turned on. It was like a night match at the KC Stadium. The Kodiak was increasing speed and so were we, Osbourne looking at us through the small cabin window. I could imagine him telling the pilot to get a move on. Faster and faster, yet the small aircraft didn't take off, maybe the pilot hadn't envisaged police involvement, never mind a high-speed chase. We were almost alongside the Kodiak. Through the aircraft windows I could see three people inside: Shaw, Osbourne and the pilot. Osbourne waving his arms at the pilot like a demented madman, then without any warning the aircraft powered down, slowly decelerating as the power was cut.

All I could do was say to myself was "Thank you Lord". I didn't fancy doing the James Bond bit by leaping from a moving vehicle and hanging onto the undercarriage—as if! We were only ten metres or so from the aircraft when the cab door opened and Osbourne jumped to the ground. He landed expertly in a crouch position, then legged it towards the fields. As the aircraft came to a full stop, Shaw and the pilot climbed down and stood with their arms in the air.

'Now!' I shouted. The driver slammed on the brakes, we leapt out and gave chase, three metres and closing. I don't know where the stamina came from, but I was making ground on him, my heart rate increased as it pumped the adrenaline around my body. I was glad I'd done the power walking, as my legs sprinted me onwards. One, two, three! I leapt through the air like a prop forward, grabbed him around his knees and we both went down on the concrete. Hell, I could feel the skin on the side of my face scrape and peel away as I went down. I was still hanging onto his legs when he made my face worse by beating me with something metal, that was when I lost my grip and the gun went off, two shots.

Have you ever heard a real gun being fired? They don't go bang, bang like on the telly, they go BOOM, BOOM. On top of that, when you use them single handed you have the kick back to contend with, it's so powerful that you can't control the aim, or guarantee that the bullet will find its intended target.

He was laid half on his back, half on his side. His arm looked to be twisted or the shoulder dislocated, and he was still holding the gun in the hand of his injured arm. Oh hell, I thought, he was looking towards me when he'd pointed the gun. It was all over the place, he didn't have any proper control over it. The first shot lodged itself in his thigh bone; the second went right through the fleshy part of his groin and severed the femoral artery, and it didn't stop until it buried itself in more flesh and bone. Death arrived before the ambulance did.

Chapter 28

The Gangsters Boss's Demise.

'Stop, stop this fucking thing, I don't want to end up brown bread,' I yelled into the cramped cockpit. I think the pilot had the same thoughts, the engine noise changed and the aircraft slowed.

'Fly, fly,' Osbourne ordered the pilot, pointing the gun at the man's head. I reached into the cockpit, trying to get the gun, Osbourne shook me off and I got a crack on the side of my head for my trouble. The aircraft came to a stop. I couldn't believe what the silly fucker did next, he opened the door and jumped out! Very professional I must admit. Just like a paratrooper, he landed on his feet, rolled and then made a dash for the fields. Next thing I saw was that copper Blackburn, sprinting like Usain Bolt after Osbourne —and the old fella was gaining fast.

The pilot dropped the ladder and we climbed down, coppers everywhere. 'Get your hands up,' I told the pilot, 'there might be some fucker with a gun.' Once we were clear of the aircraft we stood stock still and waited. Blackburn had brought Osbourne down in not very neat but effective rugby tackle. Ouch. Then we heard the gun go off, two shots. Shit, neither of them moved, no-one got up.

Chapter 29
Funeral Rites

The morning was cold, windy and wet; actually it was pouring down, the sort of weather you'd expect for a February funeral. The vicar led the entourage out of the small chapel; the mourners, heads hanging low, followed the coffin bearers along the gravel path and through the soggy, ankle-high grass to the graveside. You could hear the rain beating down on the umbrellas.

I was surprised at how well attended the funeral was, more people than I would have ever expected. It looked as if the whole station had turned out. It was a sea of blue serge dress uniforms, and looked like most of the city's stations were represented. I even noticed the Assistant Chief Constable— well he had to didn't he? The DCI was there also wearing his best uniform, with his cap firmly placed on his bullet head. At the edge of the grave, Ria stood between Questy and William, it looked as if she was struggling with things. Questy had his arm tight around her for support, she was holding a small posy of flowers. The vicar had a well-used little wooden box, full of earth taken from the freshly dug hole; he invited the graveside mourners to take a handful of earth, which they then dropped onto the coffin six feet below. Ria accepted a handful of dirt and held her hand over the muddy grave and let go, it fell soundlessly as the rain beat down on the coffin lid, then she threw in the flowers. Kaja was next, I could see her hand shake as she threw in the dirt. I hoped her and Reeta would be alright. Cheated was how I felt, it shouldn't have ended like this. I'd already beaten death and come back from the brink. That second bullet shouldn't have had my name on it; it shouldn't have ended like this. As they say, "there are only so many times a man can go to the well", and I'd visited once too often.

END